MW01131764

Stranger by the Lake

Walk with us in the Places the Nazarene Loved

by
Monte C. Fast

authorHOUSE™

1663 LIBERTY DRIVE, SUITE 200
BLOOMINGTON, INDIANA 47403
(800) 839-8640
WWW.AUTHORHOUSE.COM

First published by AuthorHouse 11/19/05

ISBN: 1-4208-7113-7 (sc)

Printed in the United States of America
Bloomington, Indiana

This book is printed on acid-free paper.

Forward

I think the only reason no one ever saw Peter the fisherman and follower of Jesus, and Monte Fast in the same place at the same time is because they lived 2000 years apart. That is to say, in character they bear a striking resemblance to one another. To be greeted and engulfed in Monte's handshake is to be taken into a confidence and enthusiasm that is touched by the Master. I have been privileged to tell you something about this touch upon Monte's life and how it can touch you.

We live in what is called a 'post-Christian era". What this generally means is that in our contemporary western culture the values and beliefs of the traditional Christian Church are no longer the endorsed, understood, accepted, practiced or integrated into the mainstream of life. It is an admission that what once was dominant no longer is.

Is this because society has not heard the message of the Old and New Testaments? Perhaps, in part, but in a larger part I have a sense that much of western culture has heard what they think is the message and given up on it.

In his engaging reflection upon the promise of God's faithfulness revealed in the scriptures, Monte Fast has re-told the story in such away that the reader is invited to "Come and see" for his or herself.

Like Jesus, there is no pretense about the way Monte unfolds the story. And also like Jesus there is mystery and intrigue that lead to hope. What we are invited to do is hear again the story of what God offers and walk in the steps that lead to discovering that this offer is personal and inclusive of us all.

For the seasoned spiritual traveler, for the skeptic, for the modern westerner who thinks he or she had heard the story, Stranger at the Lake is a map of an old land full of new adventure and promise; full of healing and compassion.

As we stand on the threshold of a new millennium the stranger who came to make Himself known beckons once more to the hearts of all. As you enter this time and this land may the map laid out by Monte Fast lead you into a wonderfull relationship with this stranger who is really an old friend and may you discover that he is so much more.

Bruce Kochsmeir
Carson City, Nevada, June 1999

Note: Bruce Kochsmeir is senior pastor of First Presbyterian Church of Carson City, Nevada, and Monte Fast's pastor.

Introduction

I cannot remember a time during which I was not fascinated with the Holy Land.

The first religious papers my little fingers closed upon were small picture cards from Sunday School. For the most part of my primary years my mother was my principal Sunday School teacher. She was not an educated woman by the standards of this world, but she possessed an amazing gift of teaching. Whenever and whichever class she was asked to lead grew... not just in numbers, but also in knowledge.

I am told that at my age of four, she had helped me memorize and recite 38 scripture verses to the adult congregation in our church in Salem, Oregon. I can still recite many of them.

When I became old enough to attend public school, our morning routine was very simple. At 6:30 a.m. I arose to practice the piano for 30 minutes. My sister, two years my junior, then came to the keyboard for her 30 minute stint. While she was practicing, I set the breakfast table.

Breakfast was usually served about 7:30 a.m.

But at 8 a.m. the table was left as it was, and mother gathered all four children in the living room. The Egermeyer's Bible Story book was opened and we traveled to far away historic Biblical places. We met men and women of yesteryear. Some good, some evil. We knew about battles, walled cities, giants, miracles, lakes and seas. The morning journey would finish in time for us to kneel by our chairs, say a morning prayer, gather our lunch sacks and head for school.

Somehow, these ancient people became very real. It was as if they were relatives that we had not seen for a long time. But they said things to me. They shared their experiences with me. I knew about their sins. I knew about their sorrows. I knew about their failures. But I knew how much God loved them... and loved me.

Finally, as an adult, I went to the land of my youthful dreams. And it was all true!

I knew these people. I knew how they lived and died. I walked among their ruins. I ate their food. I viewed the hills and rivers.

And so... let me introduce you to some of my brothers and sisters. Separated by generations, yes, but as close to each other as any family could be. They like me, have failed at times. They cried. They prayed. They laughed. They feared. They loved.

And this family has room for you, too.

Thank you

Robert A. Simpson

for sharing your expertise by

editing this first literary effort.

Monte Fast

Dedicated to my dear friends

The congregation of

First Presbyterian Church
of Virginia City, Nevada

who helped me

relive these experiences

and who shared with me

the true Christian Love

of this

Stranger by the Lake

The time...

But when the fulness of the time was come,
God sent forth his Son...   Galatians 4:4

The Pax Romana, the peace of Rome...

Alexander the Great had conquered his world. The Greek Hellenists had followed with a tribulation that sent convulsions through the Chosen Nation, an abomination of desolations. But finally, in the fullness of time, Pax Romana, the peace of Rome reigned.

It was a strange peace. Puppet kings, compromised religious systems, crucifixions, censuses, taxes, and the ever present Roman military, kept the peace, but the undercurrent of discontent permeated everything.

There were several kings named Herod. The one who lived during the birth of Jesus died a horrible death. His son King Herod built four castles and successfully fronted for the Roman military governors.

The Priests were allowed much freedom, but they knew their place.

A common language was spoken and used in commerce. People could understand each other. Common coin filled the purses, except of course for the temple coin. The Priests knew how to make a commission above and beyond their margin of profit on the sacrificial animals and grains. Their homes in Jerusalem and rich clothing displayed personal incomes far beyond the amounts of tithe and offerings passing through their little tithe boxes.

From the garrison at Tiberius, young soldiers marched the roads around the lake. A show of Roman force usually kept the peace. Centurions led their troops. Some were good soldiers, just wanting to do their duty and finally get reassigned to Rome or whatever town their families lived in. Others were cruel and bored. Galilee had its share of both.

The young soldiers, however, had no roots. The Roman army was a way to get away from home, a way to find adventure, a way to assert superiority. They trusted in no gods, enjoyed the moment of the day, and had no regrets. The little town of Magdala was their diversion.

Magdala was, and may still be, the little gathering of houses wherein a lonely soldier could find liquor, song, a pretty prostitute, and a lost weekend. Magdala rested in a little depression about half way between Tiberius and Capernium. Men of good reputation did not go to Magdala.

A smart Centurion, believing in a principal that helped Rome keep peace, would affirm the local religion. Rome knew that, if allowed to worship whatever god they believed in, locals were likely to be more pacific. Besides, didn't Rome inherit most of the gods of the Greeks and just rename them for convenience? Another god or two would make no difference, so let that Rabbi chant his verses, teach his young boys, and teach his Torah. Those things were of little importance. Taxes and commerce, these were the things a smart Centurion would use to make or break his career.

In Capernium, the Rabbi learned to play the game, and in reward, his synagogue became enlarged and beautiful. Some Roman pillars and arches were incorporated into the architecture. Strange how those things came about. The synagogue was in the classic design. A main floor of polished stone provided seating for more than a hundred men. The Torah occupied its usual place of honor, front and center. A balcony stretched around three sides of the room and could provide seating for more than a hundred women and children. The synagogue occupied a prominent elevation in the layout of the town. It had been there for centuries. But under the Pax Romana, it had never looked better.

The Rabbi may have been slightly corrupt, but not entirely. He still waited for the Messiah who the prophets Joel and Isaiah had promised. If his nation could only throw off the Roman yoke, perhaps Messiah would emerge. Messiah would be a mighty military person, like King David. In fact, he would be a son of David. The Goliaths from Tiberius would be thrown back into the mountains to the north. The Rabbi kept this hope alive in his very subtle talks and teachings. The time wasn't quite right. Maybe Messiah would come soon.

There was a sort of unspoken superiority in the synagogue. Two thousand years of theology filled its atmosphere. Members of the synagogue possessed a quiet air of confidence. They knew that somehow, they were chosen. Maybe to rule the world again. The soldiers and the prostitutes would be done away with at that time. King Herod and his adulterous life style would be given the same treatment as had been given to other wicked Kings, Ahab with his Jezebel, for one. The theocracy of King David would be reborn. But one did not talk publically about these things. It could be dangerous.

The Rabbi, being a somewhat conservative man, taught the historic theological position of serving God equals military superiority. He really believed the reason for the Babylonian captivity had been the infiltration of the true religion by surrounding heathen ideologies. Messiah would be the catalyst. He would bring back military and political power, but then the Rabbis would take over and make this nation pure again. It was a secret.

Into this very religious and political community came a man.

He was from Nazareth. There was a rumor that he had given a message in the synagogue in Nazareth that caused such a stir that the Rabbis had attacked Him with their teeth, tried to throw Him over the garbage cliff on the edge of town, but let Him escape at the last minute. So much for rumors. Here in Capernium, the Romans would keep things quiet.

He certainly was well liked. The fisherman let Him board their boats regularly. The hostesses of Capernium liked to have Him over for dinner and visits.

It was rumored that He possessed some sort of medical skill.

He may have had the best education in Galilee. Someone told about his early training in the temple at Jerusalem. He was reputed to have astounded the leaders of the University at Jerusalem, headed by the famous Rabbi Ben Gamaliel himself!

Every now and then, the Rabbi let Him expound from the Torah on Sabbath. All men were allowed to do this periodically. But this Nazarene certainly offered strange and exciting incites into old shibboleths. He seemed to speak from a personal knowledge.

Well, Capernium, Magdala, and Tiberius had a lot of characters. One more would not hurt. Just so long as the Romans kept the peace...

The People...

I the Lord have called thee in righteousness, and
will hold thine hand, and will keep thee, and give thee
for a covenant of the people, for a light to the Gentiles...
Isaiah 42:6

They were people of destiny.

This generation had not asked for any of this.

They had no idea that powerful spiritual forces would swirl about their lives for the next three years.

They had no idea of what their personal sacrifices would be.

The new ideas they would be asked to toy with would make permanent changes.

The next three years would change the world, and some of them would be key players...

To the death!

The Rabbi was comfortable with his life, happy with his eminence, secure in his beliefs, knowing that the Romans would not be a problem for him, knowing the profit that could be gained from quiet compromise. He was self righteous and proud of it.

The Centurion was not pleased with his assignment to a very unimportant post. He was a failure in the political process that could have made him a General in Caesar's army. Now he had been more or less banished to a mission that could only hold him back. There were very few good things about Tiberius. He didn't like dried fish. The Roman baths and the women who were easily available were not things which made him particularly proud or happy. Only the Rabbi was his intellectual equal. Some of this Rabbi's ideas ran counter to the temple teaching of Rome, but they were interesting.

The young soldiers were discovering the down side of volunteering for the glory of Rome. They knew that lucrative spoils were not going to be shared at this post. They were killing time, and wondered if anyone back at the command center knew they existed. They were bored, lonely, and not particularly pleased with the phony attentions of the girls at Magdala or the one recreational diversion, the baths.

Old Zebedee. In his younger days, he dabbled in revolutionary ideals. His two sons, one just a teenager, believed in revolution. They were nicknamed "sons of thunder" and well so. The older of the two had become acquainted with some of the local underground zealots. It was known that some of the thieves and outlaws that populated the more distant valley of the Jordan between Galilee and the Dead Sea were committed to overthrowing these Romans. The sons of Zebedee knew more about this than even their father suspected. They made secret reports to one Barraba, a thief, a kind of a folk hero, a Robin Hood of Galilee. They were ripe for trouble.

Simon Peter, the big fisherman owned three boats, the largest fleet on the lake. Zebedee's boys worked for him at times. He loved a good story, not always wholesome. He loved a good fight, never clean. He loved a good wife, not healthy. He loved his big house. He had very little time for the Rabbi and his religiosity. He didn't like his mother in law who lived in his big house. He loved the money his fishing brought, but not for the sake of money. It let him have the better things of life, and he liked that. He was smart, and was able to mask this from people who would feel threatened by it. He was known to shoot from the hip but sometimes he did not deliver on his boasts or threats. He could have been a revolutionary, but it was better to make money fishing. People looked up to him.

Most of the women of Magdala, as with the burden of their trade, looked shopworn and tired. The younger women, destined to live in Magdala by dishonest or unfaithful boyfriends, or by having made personal moral choices that resulted in being outcast by the Rabbi in their home synagogues, still had a bloom of red in their cheeks. The older ones had to rely upon the rouge jars supplied by the caravans that periodically came in to pick up the shipments of fish and then go back towards Megido, the valley crossroads of the highways between Rome, Egypt, Syria, and Israel.

The women had their favorites. The most beautiful woman was reserved for the Centurion. The caravan camel drivers were big spenders. The lonely Roman boys always seemed to have money, and when they first arrived at Tiberius, they paid Roman prices. The men from Capernium were not good customers. They were unreliable, cheap, and dishonest. They always seemed to be hiding from each other.

The women knew their lives were filled with danger. The Rabbi was known to follow Jewish law when the Romans allowed. Two women were actually stoned to death when citizens of Capernium both followers of the Rabbi were caught in Magdala. The men of Capernium would pay no penalty, but the women of Magdala could pay the supreme penalty, depending upon who they were caught with, the political climate in the synagogue, or how the Centurion felt at the moment.. But in the flickering light of candles, with customers whose senses had been dulled by alcohol, with the rhythms of the tambourines and soft sounds of the pan flutes, the lost women of Magdala did feel beautiful at times. And the money...

Mary of Magdala, nearing the end of her youth and beauty, sometimes sick, was so scorned by the citizens of Capernium that travel away from Magdala had become unsafe. She wished she could live her life and choices over again. But she knew that the situations which she had been dealt would probably lead her to another Magdala or another house where lust was licensed. She was simply searching for love, in Magdala, of all places.

The children.

Boys, from Kosher homes, were the elite offspring, learning to read at synagogue school, enjoying bar mitzvah complete with village wide celebrations, becoming the future under the tutoring of the Rabbi, learning the ancient secrets of Moses, Elijah, and Isaiah, impressing their mothers and sisters by reading from the Torah in the synagogue! At night they dreamed of their promised visits to Jerusalem and the holy temple.

Girls lived second class lives, knowing that the secrets of Kosher living were transmitted to future generations through them, learning from their mothers, discovering the rules of clean and unclean, and letting the ancient dietary laws become a part of their commitment to future husbands, sons, and the daughters who would preserve the genetic line from Abraham to coming Messiah.

Girls were waiting for the arranged relationships that would create a family, knowing that if they discovered a personal love, and expressed it, life would change forever, and the potential of becoming a woman of the streets would be the best case. The worst case would be to live in Magdala or suffer death by stoning.

The Rabbi and the matchmaker were absolute dictators in these matters. It was the way it had always been. It had to be right. One could not question.

The women of Capernium.

They took their religious responsibilities very seriously, preserving the ethnic separation called for in the theology of being "God's chosen people." Inside the home they were queens, leading in the Sabbath evening meals, bearing children, hopefully bearing sons, but living out on a razor edge of family or disaster.

So much could go wrong. They hoped against hope that their husbands would not die or perish in a sudden storm on the lake, or at least that their sons would be old enough to lead a household should widowhood be their burden. Secretly they prayed that their husbands would be faithful to them as they were required to be to their husbands. On Sabbath they would sit quietly in the balcony of the synagogue, even though they could not read, discuss the Torah with the elders at the city gate, or go to synagogue school. They planned for the family pilgrimages to Jerusalem for birthdays or celebrations, even though when at the temple in Jerusalem they had to stand all day in an outer court for women while the men and boys went inside and observed sacrifices and ceremonial offerings. Women could pray at the great wall of King Solomon's temple mound, but only while standing in the women's section while the men and boys were allowed to go into the ancient caverns containing ancient writings and ceremonial vessels. Being a woman was hard, but very important.

These were the players, about to participate in the new covenant, the new revelation, the new development of God's showing of Himself. These were simple people, unaware that the very center of history, the final revelation of love, the personification of God, was about to intrude into their two thousand years of a developed and comfortable legalistic system of being the chosen of God. To depart was to step off a safe path into the unknown, into danger, into separation, into banishment. And as the religious leaders warned, "You know what has happened to our Judea in past millennia when we let outsiders infiltrate the teachings of our Chief Priests, Pharisees, and Sadducees."

This would be a matter of life or death.

The Place...

*We came unto the land whither thou sendest us,
nd surely it floweth with milk and honey,
and this is the fruit of it.   Numbers 13:27*

It was a perfect February day.

The lake stretched to the north and to the south and in the haze you could just barely make out the eastern shore. To the far north the snows of Mt. Lebanon were lost in the haze.

I stayed in a hotel near the south end of the lake, once known as Emmaus for a couple of nights. It was a small but well appointed five story building. We arrived after Sabbath began, so the elevator had been turned off at sundown. It was not Halakhah to let the employees carry bags, so we were told to carry our heavy suitcases up the staircases to our rooms. Later, but too late, we discovered Sabbath rules allowed the elevator to run briefly about every 60 minutes.

My first night at Galilee was Sabbath.

From my fifth floor window, I could look down on an adjacent four story apartment building. It did not seem I was intruding, for the windows were open to the lake breezes. No curtains veiled the family activity from the gaze of hotel guests.

To my gentile eyes, a mysterious ceremony was beginning. The family gathered around a dining table. Mother seemed to be the leader of the ceremony. There were mystical movements of her hands and arms, lighting of candles, readings from scripture, gentle sounds of ancient scriptures being sung in a chant springing from centuries past. I felt as if I were transported back a thousand years, and worshiped with the family from 200 feet away. They will never know I existed, but they shared something with me beyond explanation.

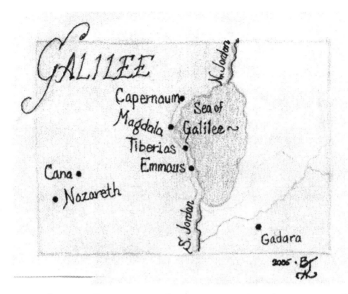

After a night's rest, our first day was Sabbath. I can recall the beauty of the hillsides, covered by the blooming almond trees. The blossoms looked like snow.

The huge irrigation pipes, springing from the somewhat shallow waters of Galilee, marching up and over the edges of the hills surrounding the lake, driven by huge pumps, were piping sweet water to many small towns and farms, making the land indeed bloom like a rose.

Water is life. And not a drop could be wasted. No vast sprinklers, showering gardens or green lawns were allowed. It was all measured out, drop by drop, and directed at the thirsty plants hiding beneath miles of plastic sheaths to avoid evaporation.

On the morning after Sabbath I traveled several miles up the western shore to the town of Tiberius. It was the site of old Roman ruins.

Romans had inherited the Greeks fondness for the baths, and a hot spring at Tiberius had been the perfect supply for a fancy Roman bath. Once centurions and legionnaires, lonely young soldiers, far from Italy and home, took comfort in the luxury they had created for themselves. Today's tourist can still relax in the hot water and ruins.

A small tourist ferry waited at the dock. And in a few minutes I was traveling northward on a lake which had been the site for a man who walked on its surface.

The loud speaker system pointed out various landmarks. The eastern shore, the Gadarenes, still off limits to tourists because of the hatred between the Palestinians and the Hebrews who had returned to invade their lost homeland after nearly two centuries. The hillsides presented themselves, one by one.

The dusty little village of Magdala nestles in a small valley halfway between Tiberius and our destination, Capernium. A prominent hill provided a distant view of a church... The mount of the Beatitudes, we were told.

The birds of Galilee entertained with their famous acrobatics. The tourists shared their bread, and the gulls shared incredible maneuvers keeping us entertained during the 45 minute ride. Mt. Lebanon came out of its haze.

And then we were pulling into the dock.

Beyond the beach we could see ruins. Romanesque pillars and stone walls stood beside old pavements, once the finest markets and dwellings on the lake. The prosperous fishing industry had its home in Capernium. The fish which came from the lake would be sun dried and shipped all over the land, as well as other far away capital cities.

Obviously, the fishing industry was a rather upscale profession. These houses were pretty well appointed, with wine presses, small cooking stoves, nice windows and porches. It was a nice place to live.

There was a pillar. Chiseled on its smooth marble surface was the name of a son of Zebedee. It had been unearthed in the past ten years. What secrets could these piles of stone tell?

The archeologists presented evidence showing where the most prosperous of the fisher/business men had lived in one of the larger houses. They thought his name was Simon Peter...

But the synagogue...

Ancient builders built on ruins. They used old stone rubble to construct new buildings. One cannot be sure, but...

The diggers have dug down to a level which seemed certain to be the synagogue in use in the years 20 A.D. through 70 A.D. When I stepped across a flat and worn piece of granite, walked on by believers of 2,000 years ago, I felt quite certain the Son of God, who created me, had stepped on the same stone. It was enough to take my breath away.

The ancient olive trees spreading northward from the lake side town still produce olives. The ancient olive presses, liberated from centuries of covering earth, still crush olives and channel their rich oil through old spouts into 20th century jars. I have a little jar of oil.

HE loved this place!

He spent most of his active life here. He was a regular house guest at several of those homes. He retreated to the hills on both the eastern and western shores. He tramped through the almond and olive orchards. He ate the dried fish. His best friends came from this town. I was going to his home.

The afternoon was to be spent at the Church of the Beatitudes.

It sits about three miles above the lake shore. One can see Capernium and Magdala from the church yard. The church yard is

***Southern end of Lke Galilee. Tiberius and Emaius are on its
Southern shoreline.***

large in order to provide space for the thousands of faithful
who want to worship on this site. The church is small, and so
groups are allotted very short periods of meditation inside. It
is in the shape of a bell, with stained glass adorning the top of
the bell, each panel depicting one of the famous Blesseds. The
bell shape provides an incredible echo. The slightest whisper
lingers for seconds. It seems like a short musical chord or note
sings on for ten to twenty seconds.

We sat in silence. Then we sang ... Alleluia... Alleluia...
and on and on the echo repeated. It was as if a million ancient
worshipers were adding their voices to ours.

We were allowed extra minutes in the church. It was late
February. The Christmas tourists were gone and the Easter
tourists had not arrived. Neither had the hot weather. It was
a perfect time. But now it was time to go out into the church
yard for a worship service of our own.

HE loved this place.

The lake stretches to the south. The palm trees and the
beautiful flowers dot the hillside. The winter sun warms the

spirit. I began to understand why he spent so many of his three and a half years here. It was a paradise.

We found a quiet spot with a rocky ledge to sit upon. We had agreed each of us would read one of the Beatitudes without comment. We could pause as long as we wished. We would go around our circle until the words had been reborn through our repetition.

Many of the group had difficulty in even speaking. We knew we were saying things God had given to us, in the very places where he had given them.

I read one. It will always remain one of the crowning moments of my spiritual life!

It was then I heard the eternal sound.

There were about a dozen groups like ours, spread about through the church yard. Most of them were doing exactly what we were doing. But there was a difference.

One group was speaking in Japanese. Another in German. Another in French. Another group in an African language. All believers, created by Him, for his glory... Giving glory to Him by repeating His words in languages from around the world. It was a symphony of praise. It was like an orchestra of many instruments, some high, some low, some string, some brass, some percussion, all creating a melody, a rhythm, a harmony with roots in one God. I understood the scriptural references of a sweet incense in the nostrils of God. We were one!

As I heard the eternal sound, I began to gather a sense of what had happened on these sacred hills, shores, and lake waters.

A reading of Matthew five, six, and seven, gives an impression of one great sermon, preached on one great day, to one great multitude.

That day, my perception of what may have happened became totally different.

HE lived here.

He knew these people. He ate with them. He fished with them. He slept in their homes. He went to their synagogue. He even taught in their synagogue. He read the Torah with them. He had long discussions with the Rabbi as well as the lay people. These experiences were the center of their lives. This was not unusual. All towns with synagogues and Rabbis did this.

But what He did was different.

Over the three years, He would disappear for a while. Then the word would go out. He is coming back. He is going to talk to us... up on the hill... three days from now... in the afternoon...

Fisherman would quit early that day. The olive oil presses would stop their grinding sounds. The women, and yes the children, would finish their family chores and begin to move from the town, the dock, the orchards... up to the hill.

And it was in this setting, away from the synagogue, away from the legalistic systems which required so much personal effort at satisfying a rigid interpretation of Jehovah's law, that had become a system of spiritual slavery, that limited contact with the Creator by outsiders, that He would create and speak

ideas bringing new freedom, liberty, forgiveness, and new life.

He would speak for days.

He spoke there many times.

He taught the twelve there many times.

He demonstrated His divinity there many times.

It was a three year long graduate level course in a new revelation of His father.

It was so radical and revolutionary, no one really grasped its profundity until He had given it life by resurrecting from the dead. Then it began to dawn on them. They had to grow into what He had given them.

No, the Beatitudes were not preached in the short space of three chapters of a gospel. They were developed and shared, in many settings, over several years. It was years later before His followers recognized them for what they were. His manifesto. These ideas were worth dying for.

They were more important to Christendom than the Declaration of Independence was to the American colonists. In fact, without His revolutionary gospel, His new declaration of love, His new path to communion with the Creator, it is doubtful civilization would have progressed to the point of developing free societies or liberty.

HE loved this place.

HE loved the people who joined Him there.

HE loved me, for when I was there, I think I heard HIM!

The Starting Point

And seeing the multitudes, he went up into a mountain:
and when he was set, his disciples came unto Him: And He opened
His mouth and taught them, saying,
Blessed are the poor in spirit: for theirs is the kingdom of heaven.
Matthew 5:1-3

"I want to talk to you about beginnings," He said.

When my Father covenanted with our father Abraham, He promised that through Abraham's children, all the nations of the earth would be blessed. Abraham was not perfect. We all know that. But when he heard the voice of my Father, he believed. Fact is, no one else was listening!

My Father counted this as righteousness. But through righteous Abraham and his willingness to obey my Father, there was to come a new access to my Father and vice versa. My Father didn't just want one nation. He loved the whole world. All men and women, all nations, were to be brought into a kingdom relationship with each other and with my Father. Remember, Abraham had a son by Sarah, that is where we came from. But he also had a son by Hagar, that is where our half brothers came from. My Father intended that all of Abraham's offspring would bless the nations. This didn't start out as and was never intended as an exclusive!

Abraham's son and grandsons, the patriarchs, actually heard the voice of my Father explaining these ideas. You see, when my Father covenants, he assures it. He directed their decisions and lives. He protected them. When the whole world went through that seven year famine, our nation grew large in the protective environment of a free Egypt. Remember, many of the Egyptians became brothers and sisters with us in the worship of God.

Then the black cloud of the Egyptian period of slavery caused us to become very dependent upon God, for life itself.

When we look back, we know that during this period of time we prayed more, we banded together more, we cared for each other more, we cared for the oppressed more, we cried more. We also built a lot of pyramids. And my Father heard our cry.

The Exodus was a new beginning. Those several million slaves, shared a mission that established this nation. Moses emerged. What a man. He murdered someone. He ran away. He lost his temper. He argued with my Father. That was how he got started!

But he also chose to suffer the afflictions of his brothers, rather than enjoy becoming the next Pharaoh of Egypt. When the chips were down, my Father and Moses had some great times. I'll never forget the Red Sea!

My Father gave Moses some laws that made it possible and exciting for the local heathen people to become one with us! If those small kingdoms of the wilderness area had been a bit more open to truth, and we had been a bit more loving, who knows what might have happened. My Father and I didn't feel good about wars or killing. Those guys chose to reject the new revelations that Moses and the judges and prophets were pouring into this world. Maybe it was coming too fast. But we wanted to bless the whole world.

We know this has not happened.

For a few brief shining decades, we the children of Abraham, possessed the military leadership of the world. You know, it really wasn't my Father's idea to have kings. But the surrounding nations all had kings. The people were going to have a king, if they had to choose one of their own. So my Father let us have kings. Under my great grandfather David, and his son Solomon, there was a window of opportunity to be the chosen nation envisioned by my Father. David gathered much of the material and Solomon built a great temple designed to bring people to my Father, but somewhere in the building, we lost it. We made some fatal mistake in our understanding of what we had been chosen to be, not do.

David really blew it. He became adulterous and he murdered. You can't get much worse! But my Father looked upon his heart, and saw something. There was a basic purity of motive when it came to repentance. David did not know it, but my Father told a humble prophet what David had done! When David heard our little prophet Nathan bravely say "You are the man," David could have stonewalled it and used his position as the King of the World. Nathan could have been dog meat.

But David was really sorry. Not for getting caught, but for the immensity of his sin. He actually wanted to die for it. And he probably should have. But my Father saw his heart. You know, after that my Father called David "a man after my own heart." There was a special connection there!

Maybe we lost it in trying too hard. We knew we were chosen. From the original tablets of stone my Father gave to Moses, we grew special laws, laws governing diet, laws governing property, laws governing relationships, laws governing work, laws governing ethics and politics. Our laws became our ethnicity. Our ethnicity became our religion. Face it, we have become exclusives. The world has become an us and them situation.

These laws are all true. Some of those health laws were so advanced, they preserved our nation from epidemics and destruction. The organizational laws setting up representative forms of government began to change the world and will eventually bring undreamed new freedoms. But in the evolution of these laws, the codifying of these laws, the growth of these laws, we took a wrong turn in the path. We used them to become proud, instead of humble. We used them to serve ourselves instead of others. We became elitists. The original idea was that we were to bless others... to be a blessing... to the whole world.

Want an example? Go have lunch with a Pharisee.

What we need to do is get back to our beginnings!

And here is where I think we need to start.

Those original guys were not big shots. They were vulnerable. They needed all the help they could get. They had no armies. They had no temples. All they had were wives, kids, and sheep. Sitting ducks in a world full of bad guys. And they knew it.

When Abraham, Moses, David, or Nathan heard 'the voice' they were humble enough to listen, to obey, and to be saved. That was all my Father was looking for. You see, He really doesn't need us, we need Him.

In our ethnicity and spiritual pride, we have become "the man" pointed at by little Nathan the prophet. We need some humility here. We need some repentance here. We need to acknowledge our poverty of spirit. We think we own houses and boats. We think we build temples and synagogues. My Father really has a much bigger picture in mind. He is looking for hearts full of dependence. He is looking for men and women who know the "poorness of their own spiritual lives." He is looking for someone here today who will be willing to lay aside the riches of life, confess an utter dependence upon my Father, capture the spirit of David's heart of repentance, and be the corner stone of the real Kingdom of Heaven, and I'm not talking about Rome or Jerusalem.

You want to be blessed? Want to get back on track? Forget the nation now. Forget politics. I'm talking to you.

Be humble. Be the servant. Become forgiven.

Remember this if you forget everything else. "Blessed are the POOR IN SPIRIT, for theirs is the KINGDOM OF HEAVEN!"

This is just the starting point, friends.

The Boat at the Kibbutz

Blessed are they that mourn: for they shall be comforted.
Matthew 5:4

Death is not final. Luke 7:11-17

Three days and three nights... Matthew 12:40

Kibbutzniks create a society of their own. A modern tourist can include an extended residence in one of several kibbutz that surround the lake today. They are required to live as the kibbutzniks, perform work, eat frugal meals, live in common quarters, and share equally.

The lake of Galilee is shallower than it has been for centuries. Huge irrigation pumps lift tons of water through massive pipes, out over the hills, across the surrounding nation. The desert blooms as a rose because of modern agricultural advances and Galilean irrigation.

A kibbutznik saw it first. In the waters of the lake there was a familiar shape. It was covered with the silt of centuries, but it was unmistakable. It was not unlike the small family owned fishing boats of today. It was an ancient boat!

Archeologists took charge, with great excitement. The boat was raised, but kept immersed in waters of the correct temperature. Two thousand year old wood disintegrates very quickly when exposed to air, and this was a priceless relic of the Roman period. Scientists considered and approved every suggestion.

After several years of painstaking study and effort, the ancient boat took form. Exact carvings, planks, pegs, seats, and a mannequin fisherman pose at rest in a museum where the modern tourist can experience the craft and occupation of ancient citizens of Capernium in air conditioned comfort.

*****

In the hours preceding the dawn, she stood on the point of land overlooking the little cove wherein her husband's boat had moored for the eleven years they had been married. Tears streamed down her face. That little boat, and her weathered and tanned fisherman, would never be seen again.

A quick and fierce night time Galilean thunder storm had descended from the hilltops surrounding the lake, whipping its waters into life threatening waves. Fishermen survived on their ability to predict the weather, sometimes not too well. More than one husband rested on the shallow bottom of Galilee.

The Rabbi could offer little comfort. He could only say we will remember him, but she knew that her husband was not famous or wealthy. No professional mourners would wail at the synagogue this Sabbath. No special sacrifices would be offered in the temple in Jerusalem. His would soon be a forgotten name. His small daughter would not have a dowry or a chance at normal life. No son would bring her support and comfort in her senior years. It was a time to weep. And she wept alone.

A warm hand touched her shaking shoulder.

The Nazarene.

He knew why she was crying before she attempted to sob her desperate story.

"My Father has a special blessing for you, daughter," she heard Him say.

"In a few years, you will learn things the Rabbi does not know. Memories are important, but eternal life exists. Reunion with beloved men and women of faith will happen. You will be reunited with your beloved. Today you mourn. But today, My Father will bless you with a comfort spoken of by our Psalmist. Peace which passes all understanding is yours."

No one had ever spoken of these things with such confidence. Somehow, His words augmented a lifetime of teaching from her observant mother. As she looked into the Nazarene's compassionate eyes, she believed Him. A warm blessing of comfort overwhelmed her. She continued weeping, but the despair was lessening. She knew God understood her sorrow, and grieved with her. As the sun rose above the edge of the eastern hill, she began an odyssey of healing and faith. She was not sure how it would be, but she knew that everything would work out. She was finding comfort.

Along with many other Galileans she became one of the growing retinue of women and men who walked beside Him over dusty roads and green hillsides, people who listened to every word He spoke, watched every move He made, and discovered answers to the desperate lives of Roman Galilee.

Meek, not Weak!

Blessed are the meek, for they shall inherit the earth.
Matthew 5:5

Lord, wilt thou at this time restore again the kingdom to Israel?
Acts 1:6

Roman occupation had its' drawbacks. True, the Pax Romana protected Galileans from the Syrians to the north and the Egyptians to the south. But life in Israel was not free!

Herod's tax collectors skimmed every sheckle they could collect from fisherman and olive growers. His fancy palace at Megido was costing buckets of money, but the Roman governors looked the other way as long as they could send the required tribute to Rome.

Herod was not satisfied with one palace, he enjoyed four. Megido was under construction. Another sea coast summer palace positioned near the great Roman amphitheater at Caesarea provided cool summers filled with the arts of the Greeks and Romans. A third palace sat high on a mountain known as Massada, overlooking the famous Dead Sea. It served well in the cool winters. A fourth palace provided a social and prestigious residence in Jerusalem.

The priests kept silence because Herod had reconstructed the temple in Jerusalem. The cost of these architectural burdens was immense. If the people had known that most of their oppressive taxes were going to Herod, with sufficient flow to Rome to satisfy the Roman governors, they would have been very revolutionary. But the priests, in league with the Roman soldiers on this matter, kept silent, and only vague rumors circulated.

Periodically a revolutionary would rebel. Angry young men would disappear into the wilderness south of Galilee or northwest into Samaria. There would be some bandit raids, then Roman army excursions, followed by a series of crucifixions, and things would quiet down. Several such revolutionaries declared themselves to be the Messiah, but nothing came of it. They were killed by the soldiers or if captured, crucified. The crosses containing their dying bodies lined the road from Jerusalem for many miles at a time. After they died, their bodies were left to decay on the crosses. It was not a pretty sight, but it was effective.

A group of young locals sought out the Nazarene by night. A traveler from Nazareth had declared this Man was a descendent of King David! Both His father, Joseph, and his mother, Mary, could trace the royal blood lines.

The men were deadly serious. Their lives could be at stake, just for discussing ideas of this nature. After several nocturnal visits involving much verbal sparing, a young revolutionary named Barraba finally asked Him point blank , "are you going to help us reestablish David's kingdom?"

Not even the Rabbi at Capernium knew such questions were being asked. In his sermons, the Rabbi had made reference to such prophecies, but in only the most general terms. Faith must be kept alive, but not at the cost of activism that could cause his death. Young men experimented with forbidden ideas, but the Rabbi knew that youth has little fear and no sense at all.

The Nazarene grew very quiet. "I have been thinking," He said. "Meet me on Sabbath afternoon on the high hill behind Capernium. I want to discuss this with you."

The Rabbi wondered why his Sabbath lessons generated no response at all. Usually someone, old Zebedee, or one of his brash sons, would want to discuss the Torah. Technicalities in the interpretation of Moses' law were always good for young ego centered arguments. But today, his congregation listened politely and remained strangely silent.

When final prayers were said, the synagogue emptied quickly. When the Rabbi began his short walk from synagogue to his residence, there were no young men to be seen. Zebedee's house was deserted. Something strange was happening. He would find out. If necessary, one of his very private visits with the Centurion might be considered. He hoped not, but peace in Capernium was important.

All morning, on the hillside, out of sight of the lakeside towns, a different congregation had been gathering. Young men, deadly serious, quiet, nodded to each other, and then sat down on the grass. Only young men were there. By noon this congregation had grown far beyond the population of Capernium, or even Galilee. There were youth from beyond the hills, as far away as Nazareth and Cana. A message had gone out. The Nazarene was going to do something. This could cost them everything, but there was everything to gain.

He began to speak.

He spoke of a deprived inheritance. Under Moses law, the land was the permanent possession of the tribes, the ancient forefathers, their fathers, and eventually their own. A system had been created through which the land would revert to rightful owners in the fiftieth year of jubilee. Such a celebration had not occurred for hundreds of years. Romans, rich landlords, and the priests controlled everything. These young men could only look forward to dreary lives of labor, small rewards, never inheriting a piece of land. This earth. This promised land. The dream...

He spoke of the glory of their history, when under King David and King Solomon, their nation had ruled the world. The whole earth was theirs. The earth, as one. A promised land. The dream...

Fire began to burn in their eyes. Their hearts beat faster with excitement. He alone recognized the real problems they faced. This generation of young men were ready to deal with the basic issues of freedom, ownership of the land, the earth, the dream...

Then he began to make confusing points. When Jehovah had called Moses to liberate the people from Egypt, it was a glorious day. The Red Sea deliverance had changed the world. But Moses did not intend to rule the world. He was called by Jehovah to invite the entire world to gather in service to Jehovah and each other. Moses was not a king. He was a man. Perhaps, after Abraham, the greatest man who had ever lived, but his mission was to serve, to share the words of Jehovah, to bring a nation, and then the world to God's laws, not to create kings. It was this kind of humanity that would inherit and preserve the earth. It could only happen as men forsook their selfish and ego centered goals and treated each other as they wished to be treated themselves.

Moses was the greatest man that had ever lived, but not because of his military or revolutionary prowess. It was because he forsook the opportunity which had come to him, to be called the son of Pharaoh's daughter, to enjoy the pleasures of ownership of the entire known earth, to suffer the afflictions of his enslaved brothers and sisters, without thought of personal reward or prestige, that God called him a man of faith.

Perfect? Forget it.

He was angry with the people more than once. He killed a man in anger. He ran away in fear for a major portion of his adult life. He hit the rock in the wilderness in disobedience to God. The people rebelled against him. In fact his own sister and brother rebelled against him.

Weak? No way.

He looked Pharaoh in the eye and told him that his first born would die.

With Pharaoh and an army bearing down upon the totally unarmed nation of former slaves, he stretched out his rod and cried, "Behold the salvation of Israel."

At the golden calf, when God was about to destroy the entire nation and raise up a new nation from Moses' seed, he would not get out of God's way. He argued with God stating that God would have to destroy him first before he could be moved away from the people. HE WARNED GOD that generations would laugh at a God who took people into the wilderness and killed them.

Meek? Ah yes.

He knew when to step aside and let someone else take the credit. He personally trained Joshua who learned his lessons well. He appointed judges and leaders and gave them the responsibilities.

Moses could have become the king. He knew that God's plan did not include elevation of men to kingship. Come to think of it, we never have had a perfect king. Moses was content to perform when asked and to step aside when finished. He wanted no credit. Only the opportunity to serve.

The kingdom that God wants to establish through your young lives is not one of this world. The world's rules are upside down and backwards. You want to be the greatest? Be the servant. You want to be rich? Give everything away. You want to be free? Commit yourself to God as his dependent child.

When Moses died he did not own anything. God Himself gave Moses a piece of this earth. His grave is somewhere out there in the wilderness. It is all he owns!

When all men give themselves to my Father as servants, then the truly meek will own the earth. Not until!

I can offer you nothing greater.

You want your life to count? You want to make a difference on this earth?

Weak people will not make it. Only those who are strong enough in their commitment and understanding of the kingdom of God to be meek will have part in this kingdom.

On the high hill above the city of Capernium, downcast eyes and heads moved back and forth in disagreement. Disillusionment bespoke the disappointment of the young revolutionaries. Creased brows of thinking men betrayed their confusion. This had been a moment for history. It was lost now.

Barraba, the one most responsible for the huge gathering, stood, anger and frustration in his face. Meekness! A profanity escaped his lips. This weak Nazarene would never amount to anything. He turned on his heal. Other young eyes watched as he disappeared through the draw between the hills in the direction of the wilderness.

Most of the men went back to their towns. Several followed Barraba into the wilderness. The sons of Zebedee, shaken to their core, sat on the grass. The dream seemed far away.

Who would they follow?

You gotta wanna...

Blessed are they that do hunger and thirst after righteousness:
for they shall be filled. Matthew 5:6

Psalm 42

Waters came forth abundantly... Numbers 20:7-11

Streams in the desert... Isaiah 35:5-7

A river of life... Revelation 22:1-2

All of his life, Andrew had wondered about things. There had seemed to be a missing factor. He certainly believed in Jehovah. The limited education he had received, along with his initiation into male synagogue life at the age of 12 were the right things to do. But when the Nazarene came to his village, even without saying anything, Andrew knew something was missing.

No one really knew it, but Andrew was a serious fellow. He plied the waters of Galilee along with his rough and ready friends, but in his heart he knew there was something more.

The Rabbi could only say, Andrew, you've done it all. Circumcised at birth. Raised observant. You didn't really complete Sabbath school, but you were an excellent student. And your father, God rest his soul, paid handsomely for one of the better bar mitzvah of our village. I have allowed you to read from the Torah many times. What more could a man want? You are one of the chosen. You are a righteous man. Just let it rest, Andrew.

But Andrew could not rest. One of the songs from King David kept haunting him. "As the hart pants after the cool mountain stream, when the graceful deer is about to fall from exhaustion, when the hunter is about to claim his prey, so my heart pants for the presence of Jehovah, oh my soul..." The crescendo of the chanted melody and the words of David were a song that would not stop revolving through his mind. He felt as if he had missed the whole meaning of everything he had been taught. Where was this God of his fathers, the One who had spoken with the patriarchs, written with his finger in stone and who had raised up the greatest kings of the earth?

"My heart pants..."

Where would he find the stream that could quench this thirst? The song only repeated itself over and over again.

Many a morning, when the boats had been safely tied up at the lakeside docks, Andrew would find his way though the olive orchard, past the stone presses, up through the little draw to a shady tree. There he would lie down. Protected from the mountain breezes, he could hear the sound of his heart beating. Sometimes he would chant the melodic line, but when the words became too powerful, he would stop, and the tears would spill over his tanned and rough cheeks. This was his secret place. No one knew the real Andrew.

On Sabbath morning, the Rabbi gestured to the Nazarene. He reverently drew the scroll from its place of protection and honor. The previous reader had left it rolled open to a psalm. The Sabbath congregation stirred in the warmth of the room as the voice began to read the time honored and hallowed words.

"As the hart pants after..."

Andrew's gasp caused several male heads to turn in his direction.

"So pants my soul..."

The sons of Zebedee wondered what was wrong with their fishing partner. He was breathing rapidly. His eyes were full of tears.

As reverently as it had been drawn, the scroll was returned to its place of honor. The Nazarene sat down in the center of the men's seating area. The women and children looked down from the balconies.

His eyes fastened upon Andrew. He began to speak of the sweet waters pouring from the Rock in the Wilderness. He spoke of Streams in the Desert. He spoke of a river that flowed from the Holy of Holies in the Heavens. The Rabbi wondered what this Nazarene meant. The crowd, not hearing the usual or familiar words, wondered what the Nazarene meant.

Andrew's cheeks were wet. His hands were shaking. He remained in his chair through the closing prayers. Then he made his way behind one of the Roman pillars where he hid, until the room was empty.

When it was safe and he knew no one would see him, he crossed the threshold stone and left the synagogue around the back way. The olive orchard was but a dozen houses away. In a few moments he was passing the stone presses. His secret tree was the only place he could think of.

"Andrew, my son. Are you truly thirsty? "

The Nazarene had arrived at the tree before Andrew. How could He know?

To Andrew, the word thirst was appropriate. Simple water had nothing to do with it. But life itself would be lost unless this hunger, this thirst, could be sated.

A hand touched the top of his head. His scull cap seemed incredibly hot.

"My Father sees your heart, my son. That hunger and thirst which you feel is now filled."

Andrew's hands and lips were trembling again. No words could come. Just a knowledge that the God of his fathers, the God who spoke to the patriarchs, the God who wrote in stone with His finger, the God who raised up the mighty kings, did exist. That God knew Andrew. That God was present in some mysterious way. Andrew knew that he would never be alone again.

Then the Nazarene was gone.

Andrew stayed under his tree until long after the sun had set. He would never be hungry or thirsty again.

Creating forgiveness

Blessed are the merciful: for they shall obtain mercy.
Matthew 5:7

The wicked servant. Matthew 18:21-35

Matthew 6:9-13

"An eye for an eye, a tooth for a tooth," preached the Rabbi.

It was one of his subtle ways of keeping his credibility with the younger people. His unspoken message was, one day, these Romans will get their due. "We will never forget. Some day, or some dark night, we will get our revenge."

But the problem generated by this five hundred year old vindictive theology was a cloud that affected people in more than political ways. Revenge and cruelty had become a daily accomplishment.

A philosophy of win/loose became ingrained in the relational aspect of the culture. Merchants looked on each transaction as a one up opportunity. They never left a transaction as complete until they had extracted a little extra profit from the customer who had no choice but to patronize them. Neighbors approached problems with a legalistic ideal, bent on getting that small advantage. Life was, after all, temporal, and only the rich truly won. By being rich, one gained a level of prestige and the money that would enable the only known life remaining after death, memories. And no one remembers a loser or a poor person.

The Romans floated above this trivial pursuit of dominance. They did not need to win on these terms, they had already won on military terms, and these Galileans were, after all, slaves, if dominance seemed necessary.

It was inevitable that the Nazarene's manifesto, His starting point, would come into conflict with the materialistic and legalistic view that came so handily to the Rabbi. The Nazarene's manifesto was a statement of humility, forgiveness, and servanthood. It was not a call to political revolution. It was a spiritual and cultural revolution that He preached.

The fishing village of Capernium, the Galilean lake region, and yes the Judean cultures were not built upon this. They were built upon pride, ethnicity, legalistic religious lives, class divisions, and materialism. The Rabbi taught that scrupulous observance and adherence to the exhaustive code of laws would bring back political and economic superiority. The Nazarene lived and taught something else.

At the conclusion of the Rabbi's homily, when his subtle point had been made, and the self righteous members of the congregation nodded approvingly, the Nazarene waited on the synagogue's stone threshold entrance. As the Rabbi closed the big doors and began his journey back to his home, the waiting Nazarene spoke.

"Rabbi, do you know what forgiveness is?"

"Forgiveness? What forgiveness? We offer sacrifices for our sins. We pay for them."

"Rabbi, have you ever forgiven someone?"

"Who needs forgiveness? I obey the laws? If you break them, you pay!" The Rabbi was getting a little irritated at this Nazarene who dared to come to Capernium and raise these silly questions.

"Rabbi, have you ever broken one of the laws? Don't answer to me. Answer to yourself."

"Being a Pharisee, you already know that to break even the most insignificant of the laws, means the LAW has been broken. Law breaking is law breaking. You cannot undo what has been done. Can the perfect Jehovah, God of our ancestors, be spoken of or about by anyone who is not perfect?"

The threat to the Rabbi's ego and his position of being final authority on matters of the religious law in this little corner of the world was on the line now. His irritation turned to anger. The pulsing of the veins in his temples and a blush of red betrayed his vulnerability to the questioner.

"What's it to you, you stranger? You seem to know too much to be a Nazarene. By what authority do you raise these questions with me, your spiritual superior."

"Let me tell you a little story" was the answer. This was a tried and tested method for debaters to present their case in non threatening ways. A good hypothetical story always left room for the other person's interpretation, and therefore had become a way that men and women survived in a land wherein they were not in control. A story, ah yes, that would help right now.

"Once there was a man. He was responsible for a portion of his employer's vast fortunes. He was trusted and respected. But in a moment of weakness, he made some serious errors. A large sum of money was wasted. He had exceeded his authority. To cover his error, he used even more of the employer's assets. He lost that money also. Finally, the debt was so large it could not be hidden or ever recovered. The man was in despair.

"The day of reckoning was at hand. When his time to give account came, with trembling voice and shaking body he fell on his face before the throne of his employer. In a moment he would be receiving judgement for his sins. Debtor's prison would be his fate for life, for there was no way he could pay the great debt in ten lifetimes.

"As the accounts were read and the employer discovered the great sin, the man clutched the hem of his robe begging for mercy. "I cannot pay, oh master. I have sinned. For the sake of my wife and children, please allow me a chance to at least care for them. I will pay you whatever I can pay"

"The employer, being a man of great and profound wisdom, knew there was nothing to be gained by extracting the last days of freedom from this unworthy servant. The value of forgiveness outweighed the temporary superiority of seeing a sinful and failing man completely destroyed, and so he spoke.

"I will not see you destroyed, unfaithful one. While you can never satisfy the demands of justice in this case, I have the power to grant mercy. Your family will not be made orphans by me to satisfy my legal advantages. Go. You are forgiven the entire debt."

"Never in the history of the city had such generous mercy been displayed. The other servants standing nearby looked at their master with unbelieving eyes. This ran against every law and teaching they knew. Such mercy would destroy the very fabric of their lives. An eye for an eye, a tooth for a tooth. It was upon these principals that they were judged. What is this mercy that our master has shown?

"The offending servant gathered his garments about himself. Tears of amazed thankfulness spilled down his cheeks. Words could not express his amazement and relief. He stumbled from the place of judgement and began his unplanned journey home, to wife and children.

"As he left the estates of his merciful benefactor, he was surprised to see a young acquaintance. "Say, don't I know you?" he said to the young man who brushed hurriedly past. "Yes I do."

"You are the one to whom I gave the two pennies a few days ago. You promised their return. I want them now."

"Oh yes, sir. I am going to my home right now. I will return with your money in a few minutes. I do not carry my purse right now."

"Oh no! You word is your word. You said you would repay me today. Pay me now!"

"I will sir, and gladly. I will return with your pennies plus interest. Just give me a few minutes. I have it. It will be yours immediately."

"No, now! Elders of the city. Throw this man into debtor's prison. He is in default on a loan. An eye for an eye. A tooth for a tooth. It is the law. He has not paid."

"When the wise and benevolent employer heard the account, he was distraught by the return of his merciful generosity. He called the elders of the city and explained that any person who demonstrated such judgement was unworthy of mercy. The sentence was passed. The elders bound the ungrateful man to debtors prison where he died many years later."

Suddenly the Nazarene thrust home the point of the story.

"Rabbi, have you ever broken one of Jehovah's laws? Does the blood of lambs or doves have any ability to pay for the breaking of a law by one of Jehovah's chosen? Remember, Jehovah said to Adam, The soul that sinneth, IT SHALL DIE! It is a penalty which cannot be paid with the purchase of a temple lamb or dove."

The Rabbi was very quiet. The story had created a theological point that had to be dealt with. He waited for the final conclusive argument. It did not come.

"Let me give you a little prayer" he heard the Nazarene say. "One that has never been taught in Synagogue school. It goes like this...

"Our Father, Forgive me my trespasses, with the same mercy as I forgive the one who has trespassed against me".

"Dear and learned Rabbi, My Father is always merciful to those who show mercy."

Whose God?

"I am not worthy... but speak the word only, and my servant
shall be healed."
Matthew 8:5-13

The centurion and the Rabbi had enjoyed many spirited discussions.

The two highest educated residents of the lake held diametrically opposing views, but being sophisticated men, they were stimulated by the give and take of a debate. The centurion really did not care what the Rabbi believed, for he had grown away from the polytheism of his youth and did not have any desire to reestablish any sort of bothersome religion. The Rabbi did not want to get involved in the lengthy process of proselytism that would be necessary should the centurion declare that he wanted to become one of the chosen. Besides, he was a Roman. So their debates were full of ideas, but no real win/loose conclusions.

Their discussions were usually private. The centurion did not really want his young troops to think he was soft or fraternal. The Rabbi wanted to maintain the reputation of subtle resistance. But they talked.

It was when the centurion's most loyal and faithful servant became ill that a real crisis developed. He was more than a servant. He had helped raise the centurion. He had nursed the centurion after a serious battle wound. He would serve the centurion until his death.

Out of the need for peaceful coexistence, the centurion had not built temples to the Roman and Greek deities of his youth within miles. The gods to whom the centurion might have turned in a crisis were not nearby. The medical practitioners of Egypt and Rome were not readily available. Galilee provided fishwives and midwives. Their teas and poultices did nothing to lower the raging fever. The local Hebrew medical laws, codified in detail for centuries, mainly dietary in nature, shed no light on the malady or any possible cure. His servant's condition worsened.

The crisis began to produce actions. From some chest of personal possessions, the centurion produced an ancient symbol of health and fertility. It was not even Roman. It had been spoils in a little battle with some pagans who believed such things. When the little stone god appeared over the door to the centurion's luxurious quarters, the rumor quickly came to the ears of the Rabbi. Now there was a real issue for the Rabbi.

The centurion's servant became delirious. Even non medical people knew that some mysterious illness was about to take his life. Nurses and servants tried to provide needs.

The Rabbi asked for a private meeting. It would take place half way between Capernium and Tiberius. It would be at the lake shore. Only a few people would accompany them. The issue of an idol being displayed in this land of God's chosen had to be discussed. It was alright to build those temples, but far away from the Rabbi's very traditional and very Hebrew community.

The centurion had the upper hand, simply because he was in control. The Rabbi could only infer what might possibly happen. The centurion simply wanted his dear old friend and servant to be well. The Rabbi wanted an idol free society. They were two people speaking from two different needs, about two different ideas, neither of which had any relevance to the real problems each of them faced.

In disgust the centurion broke if off first.

"You don't even have a god. You've never seen him or it. If you had a god of any worth you would not be servants in your own land. At least the gods of Rome are not held captive by invading armies. If I want to pray to this ancient idol, hoping that my servant will find favor with it, I don't care if your whole village revolts. I'll burn your village down. The idol stays."

One day later the servant lapsed into a coma.

That night a visitor from Magdala knocked on the centurion's door. It was the centurion's prostitute.

"What in Mars name are you doing here? I told you to never come to Tiberius. I don't want to see you now. Don't you know what is happening?"

"I know someone who might be able to help you."

She told him how one of her clients had related a wild tale of a leper being cured. The Nazarene had broken every rule of Moses by actually touching the unclean man. And he had been healed! In fact, the man had gone to the temple in Jerusalem and been pronounced clean by the High Priest himself. She knew this was true because the man had rejoined his family. This had never happened before. She had heard other stories of amazing recoveries when the Nazarene had been present.

"The Rabbi knows this too, but he has been instructed by Jerusalem to never repeat it."

One thing the centurion knew was that the prostitutes of Magdala had better intelligence than his own Roman spies. Pillow talk at the brothel had helped him put down several impending revolutions. His favorite prostitute had never given him reason to think she was lying. His questions were quick and thorough.

"Where is this Nazarene?"

The fishing boats were coming back to the dock at sunrise. Simon Peter, the big fisherman, was leading. His friend Andrew was his first mate for this trip. Zebedee's boys had invited the Nazarene to come on their boat last night. They seemed to have had all the luck. Their fish lockers were overflowing again. Strange things always seemed to follow the Nazarene.

The Roman tribune and the attachment of soldiers stood at ease on the little dock. A chariot stood on the dock road.

Tiberius from the north. Soldiers were quartered here. Hot Springs still sooth the weary traveler.

Simon was apprehensive. They could be up to no good. He wondered if there was reason to delay his landing and fish a little longer. "No," Andrew advised. "Whatever these Romans want, they will eventually get."

The soldiers did not even speak to Simon as he tied his moorings. It had to be Zebedee's boys who were in trouble. Well, it was not the first time.

The tribune finally spoke when the Nazarene jumped onto the dock.

"The centurion asks for your help. His servant is near death."

"Where is he? Oh, he is not here. In Tiberius, you say. It is too late. We cannot get to Tiberius in time."

"We know that. Our master sent you this message."

It was a short desperate plea. The tribune explained that the centurion was a leader who could give orders. They would be carried out, whether he was present or not. He knew the Nazarene to also be such a man. Could the Nazarene just speak the words which would heal his master's old friend?

"Tell your master that I will not come to Tiberius."

The chariot door opened. The centurion himself stepped onto the dock.

"I have checked you out, Nazarene. There are at least twenty persons, many of whom would have died, that have been made well when you either touched them or spoke to a God. Now I am asking. I believe you can help my friend, just as you helped these others. I not only ask, I plead."

The tribune and the solders were dumbstruck at the desperation in their leader's voice. He had always been in control. At this moment, he was relinquishing control... to a Nazarene?

The Nazarene looked at Simon, James, Andrew, and John. The fishermen did not know whether to cower in fright or make a run for it.

The Nazarene broke the silence, first to his fishermen friends. "I have never seen such faith in all Israel."

Turning to the centurion he said, "From this hour your servant is well."

It was so. The servants and nurse verified that just after sun rise on the eastern shore, the centurion's servant opened his eyes and asked for water. By afternoon, he was completely recovered!

That evening as the sun was setting, the Rabbi muttered a Hebrew curse as he opened the small bag sitting on his doorstep. A little stone idol dropped from his hands. Neither he nor the centurion had won the debate.

Seeing God

Blessed are the pure in heart: for they shall see God.
Matthew 5:8

Exodus 33:17-23

"An angel of death stands between you and Jehovah," taught the Rabbi. "No one has seen God and lived. Jehovah is a terrible God. To fear Him is the beginning of wisdom."

And so the lessons went on. Centuries old truths repeated themselves in the minds and hearts of little boys, who in good time became men, some of whom in good time became Rabbis. These stories and lessons were true. They would never die.

This lesson from the Pentateuch concluded that when Adam sinned, he was placed outside of the presence of God. No longer would Adam walk and talk with God in the cool of the evening. From that fateful moment, no son of Adam would ever see God again.

And God is so holy that our literature just has signs for his name. We do not even speak it or write it.

Men, being imperfect, must never let their heads be uncovered since we cannot bear the direct gaze of God upon our bodies.

The Rabbi was wise in this matter. From experience he could affirm that no human being had achieved perfection. And Jehovah, the perfect God, would not be perfect if he could ever be seen by a sinful imperfect creature. And all men had sinned! The Rabbi included himself.

"What about Enoch?" piped a young voice.

"Oh yes," replied the Rabbi. "Enoch walked with Jehovah. He enjoyed a special finish to earthly life. He just disappeared. Our forefathers later felt that God had just taken him out of this life. He just stopped existing, for Jehovah took him."

The dramatic gesture of the class clown, along with the sound "Poof," illustrated one little boy's understanding of the Rabbi's serious lecture. All of the boys laughed in relief.

Learning takes place at the opportune moment. The Rabbi sensed one of those moments now. He began to tell a story involving the greatest of all prophets, Moses.

In the ancient Exodus, Moses was the one to whom God actually spoke. All of our patriarchs heard the voice, but none of them ever saw God.

When Moses had been particularly faithful and pleasing to God on Mt. Sinai and the Ten Commandments were deposited in his arms for the second time, God spoke to Moses. In effect God said, "Moses, you are pleasing to me. Ask me a petition, I will grant it."

Moses did not ask for riches. He did not ask for military power. He did not ask for fame. He did not ask for any thing of this world. His request was the request of every person who is included in this chosen people. "I long to see you, oh God."

"Boys, that was an impossible request. Moses had been imperfect. He had murdered an Egyptian in anger. God could not grant Moses' request."

Instead, God let Moses get as close to Him as any person has ever experienced, and lived.

There was a little cleft in the rocky wall of Mt. Sinai. Moses was instructed to crawl into that cleft with his face to the rocky wall. He was not to turn around, but keep his back to the miracle that was about to occur.

God placed His hand over that little cleft in the wall, hiding and protecting Moses. Then our great Jehovah passed by with his back to Moses. That, boys, is as close as the greatest man who ever lived got to our God.

Weeks later, when Moses came down from Mt. Sinai, the people in our Exodus could not stand to look upon him. His face was as blinding as the desert sun. He actually had to wear a veil for many days.

Two dozen little eyes were as large as the oil jar covers stacked near the olive presses. The class clown forgot to punctuate the story with his usual youthful enthusiasm. The Rabbi knew he had communicated. These little boys would never remove their yarmulkas again.

"Is that why we cannot see the great Ark of the Covenant?" asked a student.

"Not exactly. Some of you may actually get to see the ark. Sometimes it is brought out to lead our soldiers into battle." The Rabbi looked around quickly and then lowered his voice. "Maybe our ark will help us get freedom from these Romans."

Young heads nodded silently.

"But don't touch it." The warning was stern.

"One of King David's servants, with the best of intentions, was walking beside the ox cart when we recovered the ark from the wicked Philistines and their idol, Dagon. When the cart tipped dangerously, the poor man put out his hand to steady it. When he touched the ark, a bolt of blue fire sprang from the eyes of the golden cherubim and killed him instantly."

"An angel of death stands between you and Jehovah. Fear Him."

The Rabbi was not sure about blue fire, but a little drama would impress his youthful students.

The lesson was well learned that day.

*****

Three weeks later another teacher, the Nazarene, and another group of students, the fishermen, several women, including the fisherman's widow, a tax collector from Jericho, and some younger boys were gathered on the hillside.

The Nazarene had a unique way of speaking of God, Jehovah, as My Father. He quite often used the word "Abba" or the colloquial familiar children's name for "daddy" when speaking of this great and terrible God of their fathers. He seemed to know God on a personal and intimate basis, and the followers wondered how He could dare to speak about God in terms almost as if He had personally seen Him.

The God he taught about seemed so approachable.

One of the more precocious of the group noted this with a question... "Master, when you speak of God, it seems as if you know Him. It sounds like you know Him more intimately, than... even Moses, who instituted our first Passover. How can this be?"

Learning takes place at the opportune moment. The Nazarene, sensing one of these moments had arrived, began to discuss the nature of God in ways which they had never heard.

"When Adam was created," He said, "We created him in our own image. Most of the same feelings and desires you possess are also possessed in the heart of Jehovah. The desire to love and be loved for example. In fact, if I could give you one word to describe Our Father, it would be Love.

"From His ultimate love, He grants to you the powers of choice, of creative thought, of changing your behaviors, of being unselfish. You are not simple animals, driven by instinct. You are not prisoners of a system of laws. You are children of God. You also have the choice of rejecting Him, and since He loves you, He will even allow that. But you are more important to Him than life itself. He loves you.

"I know it would be less difficult for you to understand if for a moment you could draw back the curtains of separation and see Him. And before you die, those curtains will be drawn back. Some of you will be destroyed by that vision. Others will be born anew to new lives."

One of the children spoke. "It is not true, Master. The Rabbi said no man has seen God and lived. God is perfect, and no imperfect person can be in his presence. Isn't that true?"

The Nazarene spoke again. "For two thousand years, we have allowed the laws of God to separate us from His love. True, His laws are immutable. They will never change. But there is another law. No longer will we be judged alone by laws written on scrolls and tablets of stone. There is another law... a law of the pure heart.

"Another of our great prophets foretold, "A new heart also, will I give you. I will take away the stony heart from out of your flesh, and will give you a heart of flesh."

Simon, the big fisherman, frowned and shook his head. "You speak in riddles, Master. Are we all to become laws unto ourselves. Are we to live by our own heart's desires and beliefs. Surely everything our forefathers have given us would be lost in such an environment."

Andrew, surprised at the depth of thought that sprang from his fisherman partner who always seemed to hold religion at arms length, at first nodded in agreement. "There has to be a law. This is what separates us as the chosen people of Jehovah."

"Andrew, was it love or law that you felt under your tree?"

Andrew knew the Nazarene was right. That moment when his hunger and thirst had been satisfied did not come from following laws. It did not come from any synagogue or temple restrictions. It came from the Nazarene and then sprang up from within his heart. For Andrew it had been the defining moment of clarity. It was as if the curtain had been drawn aside and he had seen love personified. Love is what his world was starving for. The Nazarene personified that love.

Andrew struggled with ideas he could not understand. They were just under the surface, but not really clear.

Their eyes made contact. Andrew felt it again.

Then the Nazarene was speaking again.

"God is not a distant Creator who cannot be touched or seen. He is Abba. He is not a hard legalistic judge. He is your loving Father. No matter what you have done that is against our ancient laws, He enfolds you in His love. He is looking deeply into your hearts, right now. He promises that an innocent child, or a guilty criminal, who prays for purity of heart is fully acceptable to Him. A record of adherence to the law is neither the answer nor can it truly be accomplished.

"The law measures your past. You cannot change or pay for your own past. It can only be forgiven.

"Your heart carries you into His eternal loving future. He looks at your heart.

"Perfection is impossible for everyone but God. What do you feel in your heart right now? Do you want Him to be your Abba? He will show Himself to you.

"One who is pure in heart will not be destroyed by seeing God. You are being healed now for you are standing with Him."

The Nazarene knew they did not understand this new theology. They would only grasp it after the old systems would shudder and die in a second great Passover, one far more eternal in its accomplishment that the original great Passover declared by Moses and suffered under Pharaoh. The immutable law of a just God would still require the shedding of innocent blood. But where could that be found? Only the Nazarene knew.

Peace

Blessed are the peacemakers: for they shall be called the children of God.
Matthew 5: 9

And the peace of God, which passeth all understanding...
Philippians 4:7

To the centurion it meant absence of war.

To the Rabbi it meant absence of the Romans.

To the fishermen it meant a quiet night on the lake with a profitable catch.

To the mad man who inhabited the cemetery on the eastern shore it meant stilling for a night the voices of the legion of demons who possessed him, and fitful sleep.

To the women it meant another day safely concluded and approval from their husbands for being good wives.

To the prostitute it meant a day without bruises or pain.

To the synagogue students it meant a nod of approval from the Rabbi and an approving comment from father at the family evening meal.

To the leper it meant a meal or a used garment left near his cave by someone who once loved him.

To the bandit Barraba, it meant a secret day stolen with the young woman who waited up at Cana for a betrothed she knew would never survive this outlaw life style.

By now more than seventy men and women were spending daily time with Him. The fishermen, Simon, Andrew, James, and John now rarely untied their boats from the docks. They had developed a desire to be with Him, to listen to His teachings, to observe His reactions to the stresses of Galilean life. Residents of Cana journeyed a few miles over the hills and camped near the lake during the summer to learn from

Him. People from Jerusalem, Nazareth, and Jericho filled out the growing crowd.

These disciples then made contact with others who did not have the luxury of walking away from tasks or were too afraid to be seen near the growing crowds. The strange teachings, the manifesto, were no secret. The centurion knew well what was being taught and the exact daily attendance totals as well. The Rabbi questioned all willing to talk about the latest radical ideas. The prostitutes knew more than most, even if some of their former clients were paying a lot more attention to the Nazarene than they used to.

The Nazarene was at peace. In His eyes there rested a confidence and assurance that most of the searchers for peace had never experienced. If one could spend time with Him, some of that confidence and assurance might spread to or wash over one. The crowds grew larger.

To those who made the commitment to follow, peacefulness was being born. To those who were afraid, or who rejected Him, fear of some political upheaval, perhaps conflict with the hated Roman army, was invading and dominating their lives.

The rebels who surrounded Barraba hated this peaceful approach to politics.

The Rabbi did not trust the Nazarene for a minute, although he honored Him as a teacher and allowed Him more privileges in synagogue ceremony than any other adult male.

The centurion kept close tabs on His every move. So far, there had been absolutely no evidence of any illegal statements or actions regarding Rome.

And so it was as the faithful had settled down on the hillside to absorb more new ideas. Again He was speaking riddles.

"My peace I give unto you. Not as the world gives. Not a pax Romana. Not an absence of problems. Not a utopian society. Not even a kingdom like our father King David.

There is a peace which cannot be understood. It exists during a storm on the lake. It exists when the Romans unjustly torture and kill members of our community. It exists when one is hungry. It is a peaceful state involving your relationship with My Father. When you allow Him to place this into your very soul, you are no longer at war with eternal things. You become peaceful. You become a peacemaker, not a creature preoccupied with the strain and struggle of your problem filled life. I give My Peace to you freely.

"This does not change the rest of the world. Those who will hate you, will still hate you. But you have a precious gift. It is the knowledge that you enjoy peace with My Father.

"Some of us will actually die because of those who hate us, but in the moment of our greatest sacrifice, we will know peace.

"Some of you will loose all earthly possessions. But temporal things do not create peace. They only cause selfishness and self worship. They chain you to things that cannot and will not give you anything of real importance, especially peace in your hearts.

"The greatest blessing will be yours when you see that peace begin to grow in another person. It is in giving everything to My Father, that you become real Sons and Daughters of God. It is when you experience this ultimate giving of yourself, and have expended all that you possess, all that you are, and you in your final moments of life, see another brother born into this life of complete trust in God, that you will experience the ultimate assurance that you have pleased My Father.

"Today I want to place a blessing upon those who would give their lives to following after Me, to following after the Pax Jehovah. Who will make that supreme commitment? Who will become a Son of God?"

It was a sacred and profound moment.

Andrew found himself involuntarily rising from his knees and moving towards the Nazarene. His skull cap fell to the ground. He felt the touch of masculine hands upon his bare head. The hunger and thirst of his life was being filled... with peace.

With tear streaks still glistening on his tanned cheeks, he returned to face his best friend and fishing partner.

"Come, Simon Peter, come. This Man knows everything about me. He loves me. You must open your heart to Him. Through Him we will learn how to serve God. He is what you have been searching for."

And then the Nazarene was standing above Peter. "Peter, follow Me, and I will make you a fisher of men."

"I will. Help me."

One by one, the assembled multitude felt the passing of the peace.

"May the Peace of God be with you" was repeated more than a thousand times.

A claim was placed against each soul that responded that day. That claim was to cost each of them everything in this world. In return, they discovered the Nazarene knew each and every individual in the group, and loved them. No matter what would come their way in the next few years, peace would be their reward. They had discovered a new truth. They were Sons of God!

They heard his benediction. "Blessed are My peacemakers, for they shall be called the Children of God."

The Well at Nazareth

Blessed are they which are persecuted for righteousness sake,
for theirs is the kingdom of heaven. Matthew 5:10

It was cool at Galilee. It was spring. The almond trees were in full glory, so heavily blossomed that from a distance the hillside looked as if it were covered with snow. The gentle lake breeze gave promise of warmer spring days and a productive harvest.

The Nazarene's mother, now in her fifties, had joined the group on this spring day. His father had died in Nazareth, several years before.

Mother and Son were reminiscing about His childhood. His earliest memories were not in the town of his parents, but in far away Egypt.

Childish memories flooded through his adult mind. Stories of a mother's fears and secrets told to her little Son were being shared with trusted disciples in this springtime soliloquy.

Mary, his mother, was of the lineage of ancient King David. Incredibly, her betrothed, the middle aged bachelor Joseph, was also a direct descendent of the great King. There were many descendants of David. Most of them were located around Bethlehem, the ancient birthplace of King David. But Mary and Joseph lived in Nazareth.

Mary's cousin the elderly Elizabeth had married well. Her marriage came late in life, but to a Levite, a Priest, Zachariah. They lived the affluent life in Jerusalem, where Zachariah fulfilled his responsibilities, actually officiating in the Holy Places in the great temple.

One of the old matchmakers, learning the history of these two residents of Nazareth and descendants of King David, had begun the process that finally drew the attention of both families. Finally, a betrothal was announced by Joseph. Mary wondered how life would be with a senior husband. What new experiences would lie before her? Usually carpenters could amass a little fortune. She would be well cared for, and if she was careful with administering the moneys Joseph would entrust to her, she would be able to follow the wise instructions of Solomon to increase Joseph's estate, and become known as a wife with a value in excess of rubies..

There was a well in Nazareth. In fact there were a number of wells in Nazareth, but this one held special memories for Mary.

When Mary was still a teenager doing her chores at that well, securing the pots of water that her family needed, a stranger, dressed in foreign garments, had interrupted her task, asking for a drink. She had served his request, pouring water from her larger pot into the small metal cup that always hung from the posts erected beside the well.

When the stranger had drunk, his voice changed mysteriously. It took on the sound of a deep brass instrument. The words he spoke were ancient and frightening to the young virgin.

"Hail, thou that art highly favored, the Lord is with thee, blessed art thou among women."

The stranger had gone on to describe a conception, without benefit of human joining, from which would come a Son. He named that Son. He predicted kingship fulfilling God's promises to the great king and her great grandfather, David. He predicted an eternal kingdom.

In response to Mary's questions, the stranger had answered, "The Holy Ghost shall come upon thee, and the power of the Highest shall overshadow thee: therefore also that holy child which shall be born of thee shall be called the Son of God."

To authenticate his prophecy, the stranger had told Mary that her elderly and supposedly barren cousin, Elizabeth, was already six months pregnant.

Mary had not been shielded from history. She knew well the sacrifices of Hanna in the bearing and giving of her son, Samuel. She knew well the dedication of the great queen Esther, and her self sacrificing bravery. She had heard from her own mother of the proselyting of Ruth the Moabitess, grandmother of King David. In Mary's veins flowed the blood of women who had served God.

"Behold, the handmaid of the Lord; be it unto me according to thy word.."

Downcast eyes and bowed head did not display her fears, but when she looked again, the stranger was gone.

It was true about cousin Elizabeth. A visit to Jerusalem provided all of the verification necessary. Mary had felt with her own hand the excited movement of the Elizabeth's six month old fetus. Elizabeth had spoken in glorious and fearful phrases.

In a few short months Mary would be separated from her favorite well and Nazareth for many years.

*****

Joseph, the carpenter, was destroyed. How could the matchmaker be so careless. He was a man with credentials. He had a reputation. He was allowed to sit with the elders, at the city gate, greeting visitors and discussing Hebrew law with the Rabbis. Now he was ruined.

Mary's parents had broken the news to him late last night. Her tearful mother had nearly fainted from the strain. How could they have ever predicted such a thing from their quiet and modest daughter. How could a daughter of King David bring such reproach upon the entire history of their families. They would understand any decision Joseph would find necessary to make.

Adultery... a capital crime.

Well not quite adultery, she was not married, only betrothed. But that was nearly the same. Joseph would have to "put her away." Mary would never be seen in Nazareth again. Joseph would have to leave. How could he remain, when some man in this place would always know his shame?

His sleepless eyes were dry. He tossed on his bachelor bed.

Was he asleep, or was he dreaming. It seemed so real.

A man, dressed in foreign garments, was standing near his bed.

His voice had the tone of a deep brass instrument, but the words he spoke were mysterious and could not be explained except by faith.

"Joseph, thou Son of David, fear not to take unto thee Mary, thy espoused, thy wife, for that which is conceived in her is of the Holy Ghost."

The stranger went on to name the child, a son, and predict that He would save the people from their sins.

And then he was gone.

*****

The eyes of Mary filled as she retold the story of the reconciliation that occurred between herself and Joseph. Joseph had actually believed her story of a stranger by the well. He too, had seen the stranger's foreign garments, and could describe the deep eternal voice. He could echo the mysterious prophecies.

They had married, quietly, and quickly. The baby would come early, but Mary would not be "put away." Even though they both knew Joseph was not the father, Joseph, the carpenter, would make it possible for Mary to take her place as a Hebrew mother, along with the other brides of Nazareth.

But it was not to be.

The pax Romana reared its ugly head. The power to govern is the power to tax.

The insatiable thirst of the Roman tax collectors and Herod's corrupt regime needed a transfusion, and taxes were to be extracted.

This time the excuse was a world wide census tax. Each Hebrew citizen was to register in the city of their ancestors and pay the tax.

There were no exemptions. Aged citizens, or pregnant women, all risked health and life in order to satisfy the dictates of the Roman governor.

Mary and Joseph had a last drink from their well as they departed for Bethlehem. It was to be their last drink from the well in Nazareth for eight years.

*****

His earliest memories were not of Bethlehem. His mother had given Him the pondering of her own heart, and these He cherished.

She told of crowded inns and stables.

She told of angels singing to shepherds.

She told of Magi bringing gifts of gold, frankincense, and myrrh.

She told of a miraculous escape by night, when she and Joseph, carrying their priceless bundle, had literally raced away from the Roman soldiers and their swords. She told of the mass funeral of the male children of Bethlehem who happened to be under the age of two years.

The gift of gold from the Magi had made life possible during that horrendous trip.

She told of Egypt.

For centuries, believers agree that He was born on this spot, in Bethlehem.

Yes there were synagogues in Egypt. In fact, the largest library in the world was in Alexandria. He seemed to have learned a lot during his childhood. He read voraciously at an early age, and became very learned.

It was only after Herod died, and his son, another Herod reigned, that Joseph and Mary felt safe enough to journey back up the King's highway, through Megido, and back over the hills to drink from the well of Nazareth.

*****

Mary was proud of her Son. Most mothers would describe their children in glowing terms. All babies are beautiful... especially so to their mothers. But Mary's descriptions of her first born went beyond the usual.

His lessons were always beyond anything the Rabbis had ever seen.

His memory for Hebrew history and law was incredible.

His insight into relationships with his peers and his elders was profound.

At the age of twelve, when he had passed his tests and was eligible for bar mitzvah, the Rabbi suggested a special celebration be conducted in Jerusalem. Joseph being financially able, agreed. There would be a caravan trip, requiring several days. It was a major happening, reserved for the special scholars, those who held promise of succeeding on to the Rabbinate at adulthood.

The eyes of the pre-teen boy lit up when His mother told Him the good news. At last He would see with His own eyes, the altars and veils of the Temple of God. This would be far more exciting than the pyramids of Egypt. The caravan would leave tomorrow before sunup.

They would burn the Magi's frankincense in God's Temple.

The ceremony itself was anticlimactic. The sacrifices, while somewhat startling to the boys, seemed humdrum and routine to the priests as they went about their daily schedules. This class of twelve year old boys reminded many of them of their own puberties, the years of study and finally, the politics that had brought them to these now somewhat prestigious positions. However, the rewards of their priestly work had led them to consider it a job, rather than a high and holy office. They went through all of the rituals, but something was missing.

An unusual crowd had gathered in the court of the men. Several priests had received a question from one of the candidates. They were quoting various laws and traditions to the silent youth. He listened intently. Finally, He suggested an answer. It was so correct and so profound that they all fell silent.

He followed with another question... and another. These learned Priests, graduates all of the school of Gamaliel right here in Jerusalem had never considered issues interpreted from these new directions. His answers seemed like new rays of light on old scrolls.

The priests began to ask questions of their own. Things which had plagued them from their earliest years. The penetrating gaze and direct answers of this twelve year old were causing gasps from the senior members of the staff.

All afternoon, and well into the night, they worked. Tired in body, but exhilarated in spirit they rested, and at sunup, the group had swelled by three times. The High Priest himself came to the temple court yard.

This young Nazarene held great promise. He was a genius. And His spirit was such that the crowd grew even larger. They scarcely stopped for food.

On the third day, His mother and father returned. Joseph was visibly upset. They had nearly traveled back to Nazareth when they discovered that his Son was not spending the nights with his new friends, but had literally missed the caravan. No one had seen Him. He must have become lost in Jerusalem. And here He was at the temple.

Mary could smile now, as she related her parental concern to the Galilean disciples, but she had not smiled at the twelve year old in Jerusalem on that earlier day. "Where have you been? Did you not know we would be frightened by your absence?" The Priests suddenly grew silent as the mother's questions brought them back to reality.

The boy's eyes connected with Joseph's. His question/reason was directed to him. "Did you not know that I must be about My Father's business?"

The assembled crowd wondered how such scholarly temple discussions could ever have generated with a child raised in a carpenter's shop. Joseph did not dispute the answer from the boy and the matter was dropped. Mary quietly led the way out to the waiting donkeys. Two days later they arrived home at Nazareth. The well water never tasted sweeter.

Joseph had been a great man, and Mary would never forget him. When other lesser men would have protected their own reputations, rejected a scandalous relationship with a much younger betrothed, and left her to the sad life of an unwed mother and the life threatening existence that would bring, he did not. Like his forefather Moses, he chose to live the humble life, willingly accepting the calling and mission that Mary and the child needed.

*****

"You see, the life I offer is not easy," The Nazarene was saying.

"My mother had to sacrifice her all. Joseph had to sacrifice his reputation. My parents nearly lost their lives in preserving my life as an infant.

The infants of Bethlehem died at the hand of Herod because of me.

"And it has not been easy for Me either. The first time a Rabbi allowed me to speak to the synagogue in Nazareth, I read a passage from the prophet Esaias.

> *"The spirit of the Lord is upon me, because he hath anointed me to preach the gospel to the poor; he hath sent me to heal the brokenhearted, to preach deliverance to the captives, and recovering of sight to the blind, to set at liberty them that are bruised, To preach the acceptable year of the Lord."*

"When I sat down to explain this passage, I told them 'this day this scripture is fulfilled in your eyes.

"They tried to kill me right there. They tore my garments. One man was so angry he gnashed on me with his teeth. The men carried me out of the synagogue to the garbage and cemetery canyon at the edge of the hill on which most of Nazareth is built. They would have thrown me over into the fires of Scheol, were it not for the plan of My Father. But with His help, I was able to pass through the midst of them. That is why I no longer teach in Nazareth. I have come to Capernium.

"All of you will suffer because of your faith in Me. Many of you will be crucified! Following Me will cost you everything. You will join the babes of Bethlehem.

"As long as you are suffering for righteousness, you will be given the blessing of being in the Kingdom of Heaven.

"Men will revile you. Men will persecute you. Men will say all manner of evil against you. It will all be false. It will all be for my sake. It will be because of Me.

"When this happens, you will remember my words. You will be filled with the anticipation of great reward. Even in your torture and pain, you will be filled with rejoicing.

"Remember, our greatest prophets were persecuted. Accept the privilege of martyrdom, for My sake."

Mary, His mother, said nothing, but from the fold of her garment she drew a beautiful ivory jar. It was richly decorated, obviously a very expensive example of the ivory carver's art. A little crescent adorned its lid. The jar was of a type known to be used in ceremonies of the Magi of the east.

She knelt by the side of a woman disciple known as Mary of Magdala.

"This priceless jar of oriental myrrh," she whispered. "I want you to have it. You will know when it is to be used."

Little Stones

Jesus saw great multitudes about Him, he gave commandment to depart to the other side.
Matthew 8:18-34

If stones could talk...

A little boy sits by the dock at Capernium. At his feet lies a pile of ordinary stones, scooped from the shallows near the ancient shore nearby. Someone has etched a fish on each of the smooth lake stones. Tourists, disembarking the small boats arriving every hour of every day, are invited to buy a stone from the lake of Galilee for one dollar.

The little boy does well.

Many strange and miraculous happenings have occurred on these waters. The little stones which have rested on the bottom of this lake for centuries could tell of events...

*****

There was a time long ago.

The community grapevine was hot with news. The centurion's servant had been healed by a word spoken by the Nazarene. Because of a touch by the Nazarene, a leper had been reported clean by the High Priest in Jerusalem. Simon Peter's mother was cured of a high fever by a touch from the Nazarene. One cannot keep these unusual happenings secret, and as the news spread, the crowds of visitors grew.

The lake was a cool place. In the evening, they came. People on crutches. People on stretchers. People with bandages. People through whom spoke evil voices.

On that night long ago, the Nazarene moved quietly through the throng. Speaking to the confused and possessed, touching the broken bodies, lifting the infirm from their pallets, soothing the fevered brow, accepting the now unneeded crutch.

One watching disciple whispered a quote from the great prophet Esaias to his companions, "He Himself took our infirmities and bare our sicknesses."

The crowd was about to go out of control. People surged toward the little point of land on which the Nazarene now stood. Desperate people in the rear pushed forward. In a few moments there would be real danger. Children would be crushed or forced into the lake.

It was at that moment that Simon Peter's fishing boat moved from its mooring at the cove and approached the mass of humanity. The Nazarene was escorted from the land into the boat, and as it moved away, the pushing ceased. A disaster had been avoided. The Nazarene asked Peter to set a course for the eastern shore, now invisible in the evening starlight.

But the danger was not past.

In ideal conditions, with friendly breezes and sails, it would take about three hours to cross. But tonight, the winds were not westerly, they would have to tack sails to work against the winds. It would require most of the night to get to the Gadarenes, but these fishermen knew how to do this.

The lake sits in a bowl of hills. The eastern shore is bordered by some cliffs. The Jordan River enters from the north, and drains to the south. In certain summer conditions, thunder caps build up to the north on the slopes of Mt. Hermon, circle around to the east and with little warning, swoop down over the cliffs onto the waters, creating in minutes a storm of life threatening proportions. This summer night was to be one of those dangerous moments.

Simon Peter did his tacking very efficiently and the boat was soon near the center of the lake. It was at that moment he saw the eastern lightning streaks in the suddenly generated thunder cloud. He knew in his heart that it was already too late. The howling winds and driving rains would be upon them in minutes.

"Break out the bailing buckets," was his order. "Every man to the task. This will be a bad one. I said everyone."

Where was the Nazarene?

The storm hit with full fury. A wave, generated by a waterspout broke twenty feet above the boat, nearly filling it with water. Bailing buckets were practically useless. But when death is the only option, one continues to try.

Where is the Nazarene?

The canvas cover in the bow of the boat was torn by the violence of the storm. A sleepy figure moved. It was the Nazarene, and he was sleeping under the cover.

The fishermen did not have the luxury of being polite. Some anger showed. What was he doing? Every man had to lay his life and strength on the line or they would all certainly perish.

In the face of the captain's anger, the Nazarene crawled to the mast, now tilting from side to side, ragged sails torn away. Holding tightly with both arms, he struggled to a standing position. With a powerful gesture of his hand, he spoke to... the Water?

His words were a rebuke to nature. Winds and seas heard Him.

As quickly as the first giant wave had struck, so descended an incredible calm. Only the foam left from the waves, made any sound at all. This was not the eye of a storm, there was no storm. The thunder cloud no longer existed. The only proof that any danger had existed was the water still resting, now very quietly, inside the boat.

Several bailing buckets had not been lost. The crew began to empty the half filled boat.

In the early morning hours, the boat docked at the Gaderene landing.

As the sun painted the distant western shoreline, the crew struggled up the steep path to the top of the cliffs.

A scream shattered the morning air.

Onto their path, from the cave tombs carved above into the face of the cliff, there came a shower of unspeakable garbage, backed up by the vilest of profanities. A naked body, unmistakably human, but as crazed as a wild animal might be, charged down at the crew. An inhuman raspy scream escaped the tormented soul.

Quickly, the Nazarene stepped to the front of the crew. The insane man groaned.

"What have we to do with thee, Jesus, thou Son of God? Art thou come hither to torment us before the time?"

High on the cliff above, a swine farmer's pens made their contribution of animal smell to the strange cemetery environment. Swine had no value in Israel, but Romans liked roast pork.

"If you are going to cast us out, suffer us to go away into the herd of swine," the wild man's voices pled.

A nod from the Nazarene was sufficient. "Go," he commanded.

As quickly as last night's storm had dissipated, so came calm to the demoniac. His tense and wild frame relaxed and slumped to the pathway. Tears started from his eyes. A member of the crew tossed a coat to him, and gratefully received, the naked man clothed himself.

The peaceful moment only lasted for a few seconds. A loud squealing erupted from the pig farm high above on the cliff. Wild eyed, the pig farmers entire herd stampeded through the rough wooden pens. As if they were of one mind, they raced toward the dangerous crevice.

In seconds it was over. Crazed animals, in a suicidal frenzy, leaped over the rocky bluff. The squealing of the pigs quieted as they drowned in the lake below.

Not only were lives lost in the lake, lives were changed. Lives were found. People who waded these shallows heard and saw impossible things. Men and women who left these shores in fishing boats, returned, and some were never the same.

If stones could talk...

Big Stones

They said unto Him, "Master, this woman was taken in
adultery, in the very act.
Moses commanded us, that such should be stoned:
but what sayest thou?"
John 8:1-11

The new disciple was very quiet. She never spoke of her past. She had joined the group after the Nazarene had made one of His infrequent trips to Jerusalem. She just showed up one day and began to listen with the others. She was strong and helpful. She asked for nothing, and was always willing to carry her part of the responsibilities that came with the growing crowds.

Her hair was streaked with premature grey, and her eyes carried a tired look. Once she had been beautiful, but the years had not treated her well.

Mary of Magdala watched out for her. There was a mysterious sisterhood between the two. Whenever anyone appeared to intrude upon the privacy of this new female disciple, Mary of Magdala had a way of becoming involved. The subject of the conversation would deftly change.

There were rumors about a child. There were rumors about a selfish suitor who deserted her. But she never told anyone anything.

When disciples shared their personal stories or told of the lives they had left behind to follow the Nazarene, she was always a listener, never a sharer.

"He saved me," was the only explanation she offered when the group asked her about her personal feelings about the Nazarene.

But Mary knew something about her. And the Rabbi knew exactly what her explanation meant.

When Mary of Magdala was younger, she was famous. Her beauty and wit carried her into the bedrooms of Romans and Hebrews alike. Quite often she was invited to the palaces of Herod where she entertained, for a good price. Once she had danced in the chorus for the famous Salome. Her presence in the baths of Tiberius and the apartment of the centurion was no secret. But for Mary of Magdala, that was old history. And for the mysterious new disciple, there were only rumors.

Some years before, on one of the pleasure trips to Herod's summer palace at Caesarea, a young and beautiful Mary of Magdala had met this newest disciple. Like Mary of Magdala, she too possessed that quality that opened bedrooms doors easily. Neither woman had shared the histories that brought them to this low profession, but there was a sisterhood between them. They would never betray each other. The penalties could be as severe as death, if a politically correct situation would ever arise. They were destined to meet again, only because of the healing love of the Nazarene and its life changing power.

The Rabbi knew her story. Last spring, he had made the same trip to Jerusalem as the Nazarene. They did not travel together, but both were present at the temple for the special feast days. They had seen each other, but there was no reason to communicate.

The Rabbi, along with several dozen other leading Rabbis, had been guests at the house of Ciaphis , the High Priest, when the discussion took place.

This Nazarene was becoming very popular. His theology was so attractive to the lower classes that sales of temple doves and lambs had tapered off. Among his followers were numbered laboring people, publicans, hated civil servants, tax collectors, and outright sinners. That is, men and women who had long ago forsaken the legal responsibilities of temple and synagogue service, were being accepted by the Nazarene!

The priests agreed, the Nazarene is too soft on sinners. The next thing we know, men and women will not need our schools, synagogues, and the temple in order to pay for their sins. We need to create a counter movement. We still have a vast majority of the people. What can we do?

Had the Nazarene ever been known to break any of the commandments? Even those in the priesthood who were not completely honest could think of nothing that could be used to accuse Him.

Then the Rabbi had an idea. "We cannot accuse Him, but we can make Him bring judgement upon one of his kind! He has a lot of sinners around. Find someone, and make Him condemn them. A capital crime would be best. Those sinners will see that we are still in control."

Every aspect of the drama was arranged. A married man was recruited. He would seek out a willing woman. They would be caught in the act. He would escape, but there would be witnesses. The Nazarene would be required to bring the judgement. It was perfect. He would be at afternoon prayers in the temple. A lot of people would see this. They could easily find a victim.

The woman should have been more careful, but when your beauty begins to fade, a customer is a customer. The money was almost too good. It would be quick and easy. And as the man seemed to relax in his pleasure, the door came crashing in. Men in long robes filled the cheap room. Somehow her garment, hanging on the chair, was ripped. The guilty man escaped quickly, but the woman found herself bound with strong ropes, partially clad in the torn garment, being dragged through the streets toward the temple court.

They hid her behind a stone partition until the Nazarene appeared. As usual, men began to gather about Him. It was fascinating as ancient truths began to take on understandable meanings.

Then it happened. The decent men in the crowd turned modest eyes away from the half naked creature that suddenly sprawled on the stone terrace before the Nazarene. She tried to cover herself with the torn dress, not too successfully. Three strong men ringed her, blocking any escape attempt.

"Rabbi." The speaker was the Rabbi from Capernium. "Today, three men witnessed this despicable creature in the very act of adultery. Under the laws of our ancestor Moses, she has committed a capital crime. She should die. What say you?"

Cobble stones ripped from the path leading up to the temple mount appeared in the hands of several of the angry men present. The woman, knowing she was about to become a token sacrifice, tried to cover her head with her arms. If she were lucky the first large stone would crush her into unconsciousness. It had happened before to women she knew and had worked with.

The Nazarene did not reply. He looked about at the angry faces. Then he stooped to one knee and moved his finger about on the dusty surface of the temple terrace.

No one ever told what he wrote that day.

The waiting crowd, not seeing his writing, grew more insistent. The priests knew they held an advantage. "We want your judgement now!"

He finished his writing and arose. "Let he that is without sin among you, let him first cast a stone at her."

He looked directly at the Rabbi from Capernium.

A red flush arose in the holy man's neck. Involuntarily, his hand holding the cobble stone relaxed. His rock fell to the terrace surface harmlessly. The three bullies, knowing that they too were guilty, and of being involved in a set up, melted back into the crowd. The crowd was disappearing. In a few minutes, the pitiful creature and the Nazarene were the only two persons present on the terrace.

"Where are the witnesses?" asked the Nazarene. "Where are your accusers? Is there no one here to condemn you?"

"There is no one, Lord," the trembling woman replied.

"Neither do I condemn you: Go, and sin no more."

Mary of Magdala did not learn what had happened for many weeks, but finally the new disciple shared her Jerusalem encounter with the Nazarene with Mary.. Only then did Mary, her sister in a former life of sin, understand the forgiveness and love that had generated between the Nazarene and this forgiven prostitute.

The Rabbi from Capernium could never quite meet the direct gaze of the Nazarene ever again.

"He saved me," was the woman's answer to all questioners.

She would eventually die for the Nazarene at the hand of a young Roman.

The Rock

Whom say ye that I am? Matthew 16:13-19

Summer had arrived. King Herod had moved his court to the coastal city of Caesarea. The Mediterranean Sea stretched to the west and provided cool ocean breezes for the comfort of the pleasure mad King. The theater, in the finest architectural styles of the Greek amphitheaters stood nearby. A special underground passage connected the summer palace to the theater. A Roman style aqueduct brought fresh water north from the coastal hills to the palace and the theater. It was a place designed for the good life, for epicurean pleasure.

To let the political environment at Galilee settle a bit, the Nazarene and his disciples also found themselves at the sea. It was a place for long walks, and long talks.

They had been studying the prophets. Each of the great prophets had referred to a coming Messiah King. Some of them spoke of a forerunner who would prepare a way for the coming leader. The conclusions were difficult to come by, for each disciple came from a different political and theological point of view.

The Nazarene had been patient, allowing plenty of room for questions and discussion, but as the day grew long, He began to ask the obvious. What did these men and women really think of Him, after their journeys, their lessons, their witness of miracles, and now this involved study session.

Finally, He put the question squarely. "Whom do men say that I, the Son of man am?"

Like school children, searching for an answer that might please the teacher, they began to repeat the stories and gossip that circulated wherever the Nazarene visited.

They knew that the Nazarene had spoken recently in very complimentary words about His cousin, John the Baptist. In fact, the Nazarene had clearly stated that no greater man had been born of woman. They also knew about the tragic death of John at the hand of this very King Herod, whose palace glistened in the sunlight at the sea.

One brave student suggested that some hopeful people were speculating that the Nazarene might be a John the Baptist, returned from the dead. Of course, they all knew that to be impossible, but that is what some people were saying.

The teacher did not correct the student, but He waited for a better answer.

Another scholar, hoping for approval, tried to think of the greatest prophet in history.

To the south of Caesarea, lay the ancient state of Samaria. It was in that province that the great victory over the evil prophet of Baal had been achieved by the mighty Elijah. Elijah had accomplished more miracles than any prophet before his time, only to be surpassed by his own understudy, Elisha. The combined prophetic work of these two had contributed to the demise of the horribly erotic and murderous ceremonies visited upon the land from the evil Philistines and the wicked Jezebel.

The miracles must be the clue. The student raised his hand. "Some people think you are Elijah, returned as the preparer of the way for Messiah"

Again, the teacher was silent.

One of the women, having seen the great emotion of love for pained and needy people as it flowed from the Nazarene, remembered Jeremiah, also known as the weeping prophet. Jeremiah had called upon the nation to return to God, had been imprisoned, and finally failed in his mission. Only his writings remained. She had a sense of fear for the Nazarene, something of a premonition of failure.

"Jeremiah?" was her hopeful suggestion.

Again, the teacher was silent.

Suddenly He turned nearly around and faced Simon Peter, the fisherman.

"But whom say ye that I am?" He wanted a personal statement. He was not asking for rumors or gossip. He was not looking for a lesson well learned. He was not looking for someone else's scholarly statement. His eyes connected directly with Peter's.

Peter was not necessarily the most learned of the group. He was a practical man, a hard worker, whose fishing boat had paid for many a meal and nights lodging for these disciples. His home at Capernium was the stopping place for many a weary pilgrim, waiting to see the Nazarene. He was not a deep thinker. He was a doer.

For some reason, Peter had never grappled with this issue. He was too busy making sure the work was done. But in this moment, he was being asked for an answer, and an answer he would give.

As he opened his mouth to begin a response, even Peter was amazed at the words which flowed out. A sense of the prophetic gift filled his feelings, not his mind. The words came slowly, but with complete confidence.

"Thou art the Christ, the Son of the Living God."

All speaking ceased. The disciples were shocked at the blasphemy they had just heard, or was it blasphemy?

Then the teacher responded with another beatitude, a blessed art thou statement...

"Blessed art thou, Simon Barjona, for flesh and blood did not reveal this to you. My Father, who is in heaven, placed those Words on your lips...

"Your name is Peter. Is it not interesting that your very name means a rock. You today have uttered a statement that will stand for all time as a great foundational ROCK. Upon this confession of faith, I will build a church. It will not be a synagogue or even a temple. It will be a living communion of men and women who live though that confession. It will be so powerful that the very gates of death and hell shall not prevail against it.

"There are some like Barraba who believe the answer to this world's problems is a political or a revolutionary war. Some believe it is in social or economic advances. While these things will always be, the truth is this confession, Peter. It is in the hearts of generations yet to come that this confession will take root, grow, and finally establish my Father's great purpose began with Abraham.

"To you who follow me, and for the generations to come, I will give the keys to the kingdom of heaven: to all of those blessings which I have promised to you. In my Name you will have great power to bind evil upon earth and heaven. In my Name you will have great power to free the enslaved on earth and heaven.

"Finally, to those here today who have heard this mystery, you are charged to tell no other persons. When the kingdom is come you will know and be empowered. My Spirit will speak through you, mysteries that you have yet to understand."

For the days which followed, the ROCK was an obstacle which each disciple had to overcome. This Nazarene was speaking in impossibilities. And He was beginning to take terrible chances, like making plans to go to Jerusalem at Passover, in the spring.

Food for thought

Your tour guide is probably related to the boat captain, and the boat captain is probably married to the restaurant owner, so it should come as no surprise that the excursion boat tour ends at the dock in Tiberius, right next to a restaurant and you have not had your mid day meal.

Food at Galilee is not all that great. Kosher does not excite the western palate that much. The absolute separation of meat and dairy products leaves many flavors out of the cuisine. Deserts are some of the world's greatest, but meats, too expensive, diary products, difficult to preserve, so the local specialty is... what else, fish.

While we were on the boat, it was a bit breezy, but here in Tiberius, shirt sleeves will suffice, and we choose to eat our mid day meal on a small terrace overlooking the lake. The menu notes the local fish, informs us that this particular species is native to Galilee, and is not found anywhere else in exactly this same form. So we order.

It is quickly served. Not hot. It tastes a bit different than usual seafood entree.

Then we learn that firewood is rare, and for centuries, the Galileans have been eating their fish in a sort of a semi-sun-dried manner. It is a bit oily. It is a medium sized portion, but very bony. Since one must eat slowly, one's hunger is sated with less food, so the economy of calories is a fringe benefit. This meal has been consumed on the shores of this lake for six thousand years.

Galilee ships their surplus. The fish are dried, very lightly salted, and are available in the markets of most of the interior cities. They hang from strings in the rafters of market stalls in Nazareth, Bethlehem, Jerusalem, and many other smaller cities. This business has also been successfully conducted for six thousand years.

A sweet desert made from dates and nuts makes up for everything. The residents of the lake know how to make up for their lack of sauces and flavors in the main entre. Honey, dates, nuts, sesame seeds, and dried fruits create an unforgettable smorgasbord of deserts.

Sitting on this terrace, eating this food, watching the fishing boats at work, seeing these good people do exactly what their ancestors have done for thousands of years, we realize that we are truly late comers to a holy land of monotheism and miracles.

A Lost Fish

How to pay your taxes. Matthew 17:24-27

In any militarily occupied country, it is systemic that some of the citizens work for and do the bidding of the conquering nation. Likewise, the conquerors must seek out and establish networks within the defeated population. Stability is a necessity.

The Romans understood this connectivity in opposing cultures better than any previous empire, and most nations that have followed. If longevity is a primary measurement, the Roman civilization gets highest marks.

Further study teaches that Romans knew what was important, what could be absorbed into the Roman world, and with what they could or could not compromise. Religion was of very little importance to the Romans. Did not their gods come from another culture, the Greeks? So what difference will an extra god or two make. So long as the natives do not get restless.

Money, tribute, taxes, well that is quite another thing.

Defeated people do not enjoy giving their money to the conqueror. They never will. It will always breed revolution, violence, and attempts to overthrow the oppressors.

The Romans were geniuses in this matter. There were no Roman tax collectors, only Hebrew tax collectors.

The Romans made it very profitable for the local turncoats. They reinvested significant amounts into local governments and services, then kept the natives thinking they were benevolent protectors. Let them think they are rebuilding their own country. Herod gets his. The Priests get theirs, the tax collectors get theirs, and the Romans, who would ever know how much they were getting?

Tax collectors had to be natives. They needed to know every person's background, family, business, net worth, and politics. The Romans could offer some protection, but the tax collector had to possess personal power and prestige. He had to be smart, for the rebels who lived outlaw lives could think of no better task than to relieve a tax collector of his purse.

There was a network of tax collectors. Not even the Romans knew how these agents communicated. When a caravan of delicious fruits and vegetables left Jericho, the local tax collector seemed to be able to signal the next turncoat in the caravan route, who would be waiting. In this manner, the skimming went on... and on... and on.

Matthew had been such a man. It was well known that Matthew had left his lucrative underground profession. The word had gone out across the entire tax collector network. Matthew had quit. He was studying with a Nazarene who may be a revolutionary. If the Nazarene's movement should rise up in revolt, the whole tax system would be in danger. Certainly the Romans would reestablish order, but would the system still work? Stability was needed, not change.

The group of disciples who gathered about the Nazarene did not deal with financial matters. One of the group, Judas Iscariot, carried the common purse, but it was usually empty. It's most active use was purchase of food or lodging when the group traveled, or the placing of a few coins into the hand of a widow or beggar. Gifts which came to the Nazarene were usually given to a needy family.

It was no accident when the tax collector from Cana accompanied by a young soldier from the garrison at Tiberius, visited Galilee. That afternoon, when a fair crowd had gathered about the Nazarene, the visitor from Cana approached them The Nazarene and the disciples were resting in the shade of a grove of lakeside bamboo trees. The tax collector network had sent out the message. Whoever can catch the Nazarene in any kind of an evasive action or just embarrass Him in front of citizens or Romans would be well rewarded.

As the tax collector approached the group he said in a loud voice, "It has come to my attention that your group has not paid the proper tax."

The two disciples whom he addressed had no idea what this stranger tax collector was talking about, but when Matthew saw the situation, he immediately knew. A trap had been laid. Just a few weeks before someone had tried to catch the Nazarene on the question of loyalty to Caesar versus loyalty to the Priests and their financial programs.

Quickly Matthew advised Judas Iscariot to pay the man his money. But Judas could only produce an empty purse. The tax collector asked again, more loudly, so the entire group would hear. Judas replied even more loudly, showing the empty purse. The young soldier placed his hand on the handle of his sword. This could be a problem.

The Nazarene stepped forward and took control of the situation. "How much tax is due? Alright, we'll pay."

Matthew knew that all the money they collectively could put together would not come close to satisfying the valuable gold coin which his former colleague from Cana had named.

The Nazarene looked at John, the youngest son of Zebedee. "Do you have your pocket fishing line with you?"

Simon Peter wondered at the question. Would the Nazarene do another miracle involving fish? But the tax collector wanted money. Fish would not do.

Peter remembered that earlier morning a year ago when he and Zebedee's sons were tying up at the dock after a frustrating night of fishing. No fish rested in the lockers that morning. And then this Nazarene carpenter, who knew little about fishing Galilee had suggested that he row out a little bit and throw the net back in... but from the wrong side of the boat!

That was a lucky morning! Not even Peter's wife would believe his fisherman's tale of the weight of the fish that broke their nets that morning. The boat nearly sank, and when they docked, the fish dryers had more work than they had had for months. Everyone made money.

There was a twinkle in the Nazarene's eye. "Throw your line in over there, John. Right beside that bamboo shoot. No, a little further. Ok. Now... Ohhhh... you've got one. Pull him in! Pull him in!"

"You are wasting my time," shouted the tax collector. "Are you going to pay or not?"

With one eyebrow raised and an exaggerated smile the Nazarene gestured to the tax collector. "Patience my good man, patience. We'll pay," he said.

"Peter," he chuckled, "Now go check out that fish. Look in his mouth."

"Wait a minute. I didn't come here to sport fish. I have important business to tend to. I want this tax. I want it now." The tax collector motioned to his soldier impatiently who stepped forward with his hand resting on his sword. There was no mistake. The tax collector meant business.

Peter shook his head, but moved to the edge of the water. The flopping fish was beached. It was a beauty. One of the biggest he had ever seen.

He grasped it by its tail. The fish gave a mighty flip and something shiny fell to the sand.

It was a large golden coin. It was new. The image of Caesar stood out clearly. It was the exact amount that had been stated by the tax collector. The fish now forgotten, with one last flip, reached the safety of the water of the lake. The prize catch was gone, but the golden coin lay shining upon the sand.

"Look at what came out of the fish's mouth, Master," young John said as he placed the coin in the Nazarene's out-stretched palm.

The Nazarene turned it over. Then He flipped the coin into the air. It sparkled as it spun upward, over and over, and down, caught in the basketed hands of the startled tax collector.

"I think that covers it," the Nazarene said.

"Don't worry about the fish, Peter. Remember, we are more interested in catching people that we are catching fish. Right?" The twinkle in His eye and broadening smile was now unmistakable.

As the Nazarene turned to the nearby road, He began to chuckle. Quietly at first, but then actually laughing, now loudly. He slapped Matthew on the shoulder. Matthew began to laugh. The disciples, without quite knowing why, found themselves following down the road and laughing too. Like schoolboys, they could not stop.

The tax collector from Cana and his young soldier just stood there, looking at the valuable new coin, shaking their heads.

Return to Jerusalem

*And, behold, the veil of the temple was rent in twain from the
top to the bottom;
and the earth did quake, and the rocks rent; and the graves were
opened;
Matthew 26 and 27, Mark 14 and 15
Luke 22 and 23, John 12 through 19*

It seemed like the end of the world.

The last several weeks had generated emotional, theological, and political waves that exceeded the wildest waves that
sometimes tore at the surface of Galilee. Like Galilean waves,
these more potent waves had taken innocent lives. There had
been riots during Passover in Jerusalem. The pax Romana was
in jeopardy. Pilot, the Roman governor had proven very inef-
fective. His wife had gone insane. The very foundation stones
of the temple itself had been shaken by an earthquake. The
veil in the temple suffered a great tear. Sepulchers and tombs
had been opened. Barraba, the notorious outlaw, had been
freed from the Roman prison. An unpredicted eclipse had
occurred. And the Nazarene was dead!

*****

It had started several months before, when the Nazarene
had given instructions that His followers would celebrate the
Passover in Jerusalem.

The arguments against such folly were unanimous. The
tax collectors, the Rabbis, the Priests, the Roman governors,
they were in control in Jerusalem. This would be no place
for a controversial and charismatic Nazarene to show Himself.
But his face was set towards Jerusalem and Passover.

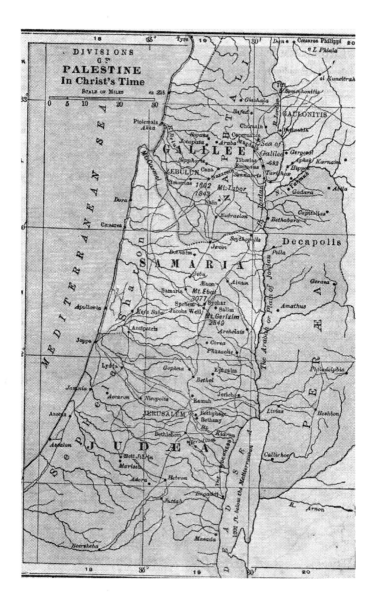

*****

Bethany, is a nice little village on the eastern slope of the Mt. of Olives, close to Jerusalem.

As they drew close to Bethany, the Nazarene gave some strange instructions.

"Go into the village. There you will find an ass and her colt tied. Bring them to me. If the owner asks you anything, just say the master needs them. He will send them without trouble."

Sure enough, it happened exactly as He had instructed.

When they were within view of the ancient and beautiful city of David, He spread a blanket on the still untrained and unbroken colt. Strangely, the animal waited quietly and accepted his burden without complaint.

There is a Golden Gate, built into the eastern wall of the city. It was reserved to returning heros, or visiting dignitaries. Historically, it was known as the gate through which King David, riding on a donkey, had entered his capital to be crowned king of the ancient kingdom of Israel.

The Nazarene's caravan took the route leading to the Golden Gate.

Jerusalem, the Judean capital, was a city full of spies. Intrigue ruled. The citizens of Jerusalem knew the Nazarene was nearby before they could see Him. The news swept through the city like a fire. He is coming. He is coming on a donkey. He is planning to enter through the Golden Gate.

Every Passover visitor, people from far away villages, even foreigners, wanted to see this stranger from the lake of Galilee. The rumor had spread like a wild fire, "He is an offspring of King David. He has power with God that no prophet, priest or king has had for centuries We may be seeing history in the making. The Romans may be in for the surprise of their lives."

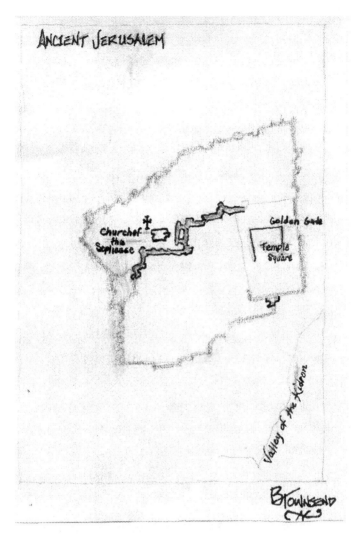

ANCIENT JERUSALEM

Church of
the
Sepluese

Golden Gate

Temple
Square

Valley of the Kidron

B TOWNSEND

They rushed to the Kidron valley avenue leading to the gate. The walls above the Golden Gate were jammed with citizens and tourists.

And then the donkey came into view.

The spark that ignited the hysterical explosion was a palm branch. Perhaps a boy had climbed the tree for a better look? Perhaps the branch was about to fall off anyhow? But as the donkey crossed the little brook at the bottom of the hill, just before the road begins to climb back up to the Golden Gate, the palm branch fell.

An old man picked it up and waved it back and forth.

The symbolism was unmistakable. Every child knew what should happen when a king is crowned. Within minutes palm branches appeared everywhere. The palms produced the same effect as the outlawed blue and white Star of David flag would have produced. A mighty army of Judean citizens, unified under the flag of the palm tree had been created in seconds.

The little colt stepped over the creek and began the trip up the hill to the city. Ten thousand people lined the parapets of the eastern wall of the city. Additional thousands spilled out of the surrounding small gates and windows, flooding down onto the path. The mighty cheer turned into a roar which could be heard for miles, but more importantly in the Roman garrison next to the Temple a half mile away. The High Priest Caiphas heard it from his private residence. Priests and soldiers knew a day of reckoning was at hand. The path up to the Golden Gate was no longer surfaced by rutted cobblestone, it was covered with the garments of adoring and excited people.

"He is David's son. Hosanna to the One who comes in the name of David. Hosanna to the One who comes in the name of our God!" chanted the happy throng. The sound rose and fell as might a national anthem. Women danced the ancient dances of Miriam. Children threw flowers. David's son was definitely entering the city of His ancestor, riding on the symbolic donkey, and Passover just a week away. God was about to deliver them. They knew it.

The road which enters at the Golden Gate travels but a short distance and then leads to the temple mound. The centerpiece of Israel's universe rested upon that spot. The Holy Temple.

People swarmed like bees up the temple mound sides. Before the donkey could get into the courtyard of the temple, it was jammed with jubilant people. Psalms of deliverance began to fill the air as the crowd pushed back making room for the donkey and its famous rider. The Nazarene dismounted and saying nothing, entered the temple. Who knew what he might be wearing when he came out?

The duty priest, charged with the daily sacrifices, was nervous. This could turn ugly in minutes.

"Can you make them calm down a bit. This shouting and noise are not proper in this place," he addressed the Nazarene.

"This must happen," was the reply. "If I told them to stop praising God, the stones would begin to cry out."

Now that the Nazarene was inside the thick stone walls of the temple, he could hear another sound. The crying of sheep, the lowing of cattle, the cooing of doves was loud enough to notice even in the din of the wild celebration.

Along the wall of the room were a series of booths. Every item needed for the sacrificial ceremonies was on display. Tables and signs showed grains, wines, oils, accompanying displays showing the perfect inspection rules for the doves, sheep, bullocks, and oxen lined the room. All of these booths and cages presented the opportunity for the worshiper to secure the necessary ceremonial items, but at very high prices. Cages held the animals. Cash boxes stood ready to change coin of the realm into coin of the temple. This money changing also created a profit. The apprentice priests were gaining valuable experience in retail sales and money handling, learning how to become wealthy leaders in this econo-religion.

Below the temple mound, out of site and to the rear, a stockyard of holding pens were filled with the larger animals. They were brought in from the Levitical farms. It was the low-

ing of these animals echoing up the stairways that the Nazarene could hear.

Citizens had learned the hard way that the best animal they could select from their own flock, no matter how carefully raised and fed, would not pass inspection by the priest. Some flaw would be found. The only way to meet one's obligation was to purchase, at very high prices with temple coin, the necessary animal or items from the priests. Citizens were not dumb. They suspected the animals they were purchasing were as flawed as the carefully nurtured animals from their own villages and farms. They knew they were being doubly gouged. They were filled with resentment, but whatever the priests required had to be satisfied.

The Nazarene looked about. "I came here to pray," He said. "Who can pray in this place? It is a den of thieves."

From one of the booths he picked up a used rope. It made an excellent whip. The cage full of doves was the first casualty. It crashed to the floor, breaking open. The flock of birds flew about the room in panic. The money boxes were not to be spared. Crashing to the floor, temple coin and Roman coin mixed in a mess of broken tables, boxes, and untied and bleating, frightened small animals.

The on duty priest ran from the room in panic. Someone had to put a stop to this vandalism. But before he could return, the Nazarene had completed his task, moved out the side entrance away from the crowd, descending from the Temple mound down the western path.

Soon He was traveling back to his lodging in Bethany.

*****

The home of Simon of Bethany, a leper who had been healed by the Nazarene, was a good place to stay. Several other close friends lived in Bethany. The twelve closest disciples, Mary his mother, Mary of Magdala, and a few others of His closest friends had made the trip.

Simon offered to host a dinner in honor of the Nazarene. The guest list was made up of disciples and friends. Some journeyed up the hill from Jerusalem. Cana being only a day away, the wine grape grower came. He brought one of his best vintages. As the evening wore on and the guests grew mellow in the comfort of Simon's hospitality, testimonies and stories were shared.

The quiet woman sitting in the shadows near the window was listening to the quiet worshipful recollections, the happy and sad stories, sharing the laughter and love of the evening.

When the evening was about to end, she arose from her corner and approached the couch on which the Nazarene was lounging. From a bag hanging at her waist, she took a small jar. It was made of alabaster with beautiful carvings of floral displays. It was so fragile that it was transparent in the lamp light.

Approaching Him from behind, she was visible to all in the room. She extended her hands above His head. Suddenly, it was very still.

The fragile beauty of the alabaster container crushed with hardly a sound. The unmistakable fragrance of a rare perfumed ointment filled the air as the very expensive cosmetic dripped from her fingers to his hair. Tears were streaming down her face as she knelt before Him.

"You saved me," was all she said.

The room, heavy with the perfume of the ointment, was deathly still. The gift was so extravagant, so expensive, that it must have taken years for her to gather the money needed to purchase such a treasure. It was her life that she was breaking before Him and all present. It was her all.

Silently, the guests gathered their cloaks and made their separate ways to their lodging for the night. She too, was gone. Only a few disciples and Simon the former leper remained.

Judas Iscariot, the holder of the purse, cleared his throat.

"Master," he said. "That was incredible. But why did you let her do that. Think of the good we could have done if we had just accepted the gift and sold it. Why it would have provided food and care for several families for many months."

The Nazarene answered quietly, "Do not trouble this woman. She has brought forth a good work for Me. We will always have poor people to care for. But you will not always see Me. She poured this ointment over my head and beard for my burial. This was such an important gift that wherever the good news I have given to you is shared, the story of this woman's gift and her worship will be told. It will be an eternal memorial, not just to me, but to her also."

Judas had another set of values. He did not agree with the Nazarene at all.

The next day he kept his appointment with the Chief Priest. There he learned that there was a reward for the Nazarene because of the temple riot. Judas was now certain the Nazarene would never accomplish his potential. Another chance to establish the kingdom of David had been lost because the Nazarene was afraid, or unbalanced, or a lost cause. Money and power could have belonged to all of them, but the Nazarene had thrown the once in a lifetime opportunity away.

Judas also knew the priest could not take any real punitive actions. The priests had no legal judicial powers. But maybe they could get the Nazarene to understand the way things really were. It would be better to work through the priests than the Romans.

The next day, the quiet woman left the entourage, and returned to Mary of Magdala's little house at Galilee. She knew she would be spotted in Jerusalem.

*****

There followed a week of the most intense teaching the disciples had known. It was so symbolic, filled with such parables and metaphors, that they only became more confused. But they all listened.

He was talking about death. He was talking about Jonah and three days. He was talking about virgins and weddings. He was talking about investing talents. He talked about the hypocrisy of scribes and pharisees. He spoke in apocalyptic statements about wars and rumors of wars. He spoke of false prophets. He spoke about persecution of great prophets. He spoke of coming tribulations. It was all so overwhelming.

For many years they would discuss these things, and only in hind sight would they ever be able to begin to understand.

*****

Each follower brought a different personality and perspective to the group.

There was John, son of Zebedee. He was just out of his teens. He was a romantic soul, believing in the higher values of men and women. He always stayed very close to the Nazarene.

Two of the disciples were men of action. They did not give much time for theology. They were doers. Simon Peter was one. Judas Iscariot was the other.

In his quiet manner, Andrew only desired to please God.

Matthew, an accountant tax collector, wanted things to be correct. He was known to keep a diary.

Mary of Magdala. Ever the servant, anticipating the slightest need of the Nazarene.

Mary and Martha, sisters of Lazarus, recently the recipient of a miracle.

Mary, His Mother.

The majority were Galileans, fishermen.

None of them were scholars or priests. There were no Levites. Simple, working class men and women.

The culture of that day, hence the accounts which they later wrote down, did not address women as leaders or disciples. But the teaching of the Nazarene, and his close association with many women gives reason to believe He considered them as disciples, equal in their devotion and love as any of the men.

It was with this group He planned to celebrate the happiest of the great Judean festivals, Passover.

They would not celebrate in the relative security of Simon, the leper's Bethany home. They would go directly to the center of the religious establishment, Jerusalem.

A room was secured near the Pools of Bethesda. They had seen this room several years before when the Nazarene had healed a crippled man by these same pools.

The Nazarene arrived before anyone else. As the others entered, He was waiting with a basin of water. A towel covered his shoulders. Each guest was asked to be seated, the Nazarene knelt before Him or her, and massaged their feet in the cool water. Then using his towel, He placed their feet back into sandals. It was a traveling courtesy afforded to high ranking guests, usually performed by the most humble servant.

When Peter arrived and saw what was about to happen, he rebelled. "Master, you will never wash my feet!"

"If you refuse me, you will have no part in my kingdom, good fisherman," was the reply.

"If a kingdom it is to be, then wash my hands and face, too," Peter responded in exaggerated tone.

As the sun set, and the Thursday night ceremonies began, disciples placed the blood of the pascal lamb over the door posts, closed the door tightly, and began the night of remembrance. Tomorrow would be Friday and then the Sabbath.

They were still reeling from the experiences of the week. The near riot at the Golden Gate, the moment of real anger in the temple itself, the formal dinner at Simon the leper's house, the week of study, and now this climactic religious feast. It had been a series of highs and lows unlike anything they had ever experienced. Not even the thrill rides on the Lake of Galilee in a storm caused such emotions.

"Why is this night like unto no other night..." The ancient passages and ceremonies began.

The night was made solemn by the use of the lambs blood, but there was a sense of freedom that undergirded the solemnity. Their ancestors had been delivered from slavery on this night. God had done a horrible miracle. Death had come to the oppressors, but freedom to the slaves. As long as they could eat this meal, there was hope. The night was a celebration of that hope. But Judas Iscariot was not thinking of ancient Egyptians. He was thinking about Romans.

The words were said. The strange tasting food was consumed. The meal was completed. Usually it was time to retire and this night was not a night to be outside. The sealed protection of the hyssop smeared blood required they wait until the dawning of the morning light.

The Nazarene had been quiet, letting the other men say the words as the ceremonies progressed. Now as the benediction was about to be spoken, he interrupted. There was a great sadness in his tone and physical body. In a voice filled with emotion he said,

"One of you is about to betray me. The one who dips his hand into the dish is the one."

Judas Iscariot involuntarily gasped as he realized his hand was in the same dish as the Nazarene's.

"Is it I?" he whispered.

"What you have to do, do quickly," was the Nazarene's whispered response.

Moments later, Judas departed through a side entrance and found himself outside the room, alone in the deserted city street on the night of Passover.

"Does anyone have a weapon?" the Nazarene suddenly asked.

Peter, always the man of action, showed his fisherman's knife. It was razor sharp. Larger than a dagger, but shorter than a sword, it was a useful tool in an emergency on the lake. It could cut through ropes, or wood, if necessary.

The Nazarene called for wine and bread. The owner of the room was prepared for anything, and soon served the requested items.

"I am giving you a new promise, a new covenant, a new last will and testament," the Nazarene said. Why did His voice sound so distant, so eternal? They had never heard Him speak or sound like this.

With a cracking sound, He broke the hard unleavened loaf of ceremonial bread.

"This bread is my body . Take it. Eat it."

The silence of the room was broken only by the cracking sound of unleavened bread being broken into smaller pieces. This was not a part of the Passover ceremony. The disciples looked at each other, but then averted their gaze. Bread? His body? What can this mean?

They heard the sound of a liquid being poured.

When they looked up, a simple pottery chalice was held high above his head.

"All of you... Drink it."

The cup passed from hand to hand. He refilled it several times.

His voice, again sounding distant and eternal, broke into the silence.

"This is my blood of the new will and testament. It is shed for many for the remission of sins."

When the cup finally returned to the table he spoke again.

"I covenant with you all. I will not drink henceforth of the fruit of the vine until I drink it new with you in My Father's kingdom."

One of the women began to sing a familiar Psalm written by the greatest of their prophets, Isaiah. She was thinking about the first Passover called by Moses, but Isaiah had seen another and final celebration.

He was wounded for our transgressions,
He was bruised for our iniquities,
The chastisement of our peace was upon Him,
And with His stripes we are healed.

All we like Sheep have gone astray,
We have turned every one unto his own way;
And the Lord...
      Hath laid upon Him the iniquity of us all.

He was oppressed,
He was afflicted,
Yet He opened not his mouth...

When the sound of her voice faded away, the Nazarene moved to the forbidden door. Reluctantly, but together the group moved out of the room into the dark Passover night. He was rewriting all of the rules.

"You will be scattered like sheep tonight," He was saying. "But let us meet back at Galilee."

They exited the city walls through a small emergency door built beside the now famous Golden Gate and began to retrace their steps away from the city.

Peter fingered his scabbard. The razor sharp fish knife was ready. "I will not be scattered. If everyone else leaves, I'll still be here," he said determinedly.

One by one the others nodded in assent. "You can count on us. We would rather die than leave you!"

As they crossed the brook that had been the scene of the famous donkey ride, towards an ancient olive grove, the Nazarene looked at Peter.

"Before the rooster crows, you will deny me three times."

The Rooster's Song

He began to curse, and to swear, saying,
"I know not the man." And immediately the cock crew.
Matthew 26:69 through 27:5

His scabbard and fisherman's knife rested in the bottom of the pool of Bethesda. If anyone recognized him, it could be the end of his life.

He really thought the Nazarene meant him to use that knife, but when he had drawn it, in fact when he had taken a vicious swing at that soldier's head, the Nazarene had shown irritation. "Put away your sword, Peter. It is not the time for that."

It was then he had run.

Now he was standing near a little stand holding a metal basket in which a fire burned. The spring night air was cold. Several people, like him, were warming their hands. No daylight painted the eastern sky yet.

Inside the High Priest's mansion something was happening. Several lessor priests had just entered. Rousted from their beds by Roman soldiers, they had been summoned here. Their opinions were needed. Suddenly another carriage clattered to a stop. It was the royal coach of Herod. The guards came to attention as the puppet King walked across the spacious marble porch and into the mansion.

Peter, the fisherman from Galilee, was having a hard time trying to look inconspicuous. Where had all of the other disciples gone? Was he the only one who was willing to risk finding out what was happening? The night people of Jerusalem had let Peter overhear their gossip. The Nazarene might be held in the High Priest's mansion at this very moment. Peter meant to find out.

"What's your name, fisherman? Aren't you with the Nazarene?" a little servant girl who had come out of the mansion asked.

"I don't know what you are talking about," replied Peter.

She ran back into the mansion. In a few seconds, another servant girl came out.

This time Peter's heart was filled with fear. This girl looked familiar.

She recognized Peter instantly. "You were with Him earlier, weren't you? I remember, you were at the parade."

From his past, a forgotten fisherman's oath escaped his lips. "I never knew this man."

The girl looked at him strangely and then retreated back into the mansion.

Alone now, with the two street people, Peter pulled his cloak about himself. It would do no good at all for him to be arrested right now.

The stranger who shared the warmth of the fire looked at Peter quizzically.

"You are from Galilee though, aren't you. I can tell by your accent. Everyone at Galilee knew this man. What can you tell us about Him?"

A past that Peter had nearly forgotten asserted itself. It was a classic reversion.

His fists doubled up, ready for anything. Foul fisherman's curses and oaths filled the cold Passover night air as Peter lied to this unimportant stranger.

The stranger quickly stepped back, away from the fire, poised on the balls of his feet, ready to dodge anything should this fisherman loose complete control.

A curtain in the upstairs window fluttered. Peter glanced up just in time to see the seamless robe of the Nazarene standing between two soldiers, near that window. The Nazarene had heard every profanity, every untrue word.

At that moment, a sleepy rooster began his serenade to the coming sun. Friday was about to dawn.

*****

Peter was running again.

He was running away from this terrible city. Down towards the brook he ran. Through the olive grove, wherein the last moments of his discipleship had ended. Through a graveyard.

His blood ran cold as he saw the body. It was hanging from an olive tree. It still was swinging gently from the death struggle that had just occurred. This man had committed suicide, and just minutes before.

How Peter wished it could have been him.

He stopped his flight to look at the man.

It was his friend, Judas Iscariot!

A cry tore from Peter's throat. Convulsive sobs shook his exhausted body. Bitter tears flowed until there were no more tears in his body. His eyes were now dry, but Peter still sobbed, as the roosters of Jerusalem brought the city to life. Their raucous song took on the rhythm of the curses that would haunt Peter's dreams for weeks.

The horrible but eternal day was about to dawn.

"Why is this night unlike all others..." would take on a whole new meaning.

Myrrh

And many women were there beholding afar off, ...
ministering unto Him:

Matthew 27:55-56

He was dead. There was no question about it.

The body laid on a flat rocky outcropping about halfway down the hill known as Golgotha, or the place of the skull. It had been rather unceremoniously placed there by the soldiers. Jewish leaders had raised the issue of his being left on the cross past sundown. Sabbath would begin at sundown. The Romans did not care and might have left the body hanging there for days or weeks.. But if His friends wanted his body, they could come and get it.

Only a few women remained.

Mary of Magdala could not tear herself away. She had seen the agony of the Nazarene's Mother, now safely in the care of young John. The mother of Zebedee's sons lingered nearby.

Mary knelt beside the lifeless body. If she had not remained nearby during the entire execution, had seen the floggings, watched the thorns crushed deep into his forehead, shuddered at the torture when they had plucked his beard from his face, and observed the final thrust of the tribune's spear, she would not have recognized Him at all.

From the little bag which she used as a purse, she removed a beautiful container. It was wrought of pure ivory. A little crescent decorated the top. It was the coat of arms of a Magi from a far eastern country. Carefully she opened the little treasure.

The scent of a very old container of spice, myrrh, escaped.

Most of the liquid, more than thirty years old, had evaporated, leaving something of a salve.

Using the cloth that had wrapped the container, she tried to cleanse the mangled face by rubbing it with the salve. Dirt, sweat, blood, and water mingled with the old embalming spice. Her streaming tears mixed with the salve and the Nazarene's blood. The thorns that she could not remove from his brow tore at her fingers and pierced the little cloth.

"Won't someone help me," she cried. Old Zebedee's weeping wife pulled in vain at Mary's cloak.

When the small amount of salve was exhausted, she continued to try to cleanse the lifeless Nazarene. But there was no time. She did not have a proper burial cloth. She did not have the necessary cleansing basins. She would come back later, if they would let her.

As the sun began to set, her companion pulled her away. They had to be in a safer place before Sabbath. As the last rays of the sun were disappearing , a secret disciple came, wrapped the body in a shroud and placed it in his own newly excavated grave at the bottom of Golgotha.

Strangers at the Lake

Peter ... said unto Him, "Lord, thou knowest all things;":
John 20 and 21

Peter had heard a lot. He had seen nothing.

In the nick of time, just before sundown, Joseph of Arimethaea had claimed the body. Joseph's own tomb had been recently constructed near the base of the hill on which the crucifixion had taken place. The body was placed in Joseph's new tomb with minutes to spare. Preparations would have to wait until after Sabbath. A huge stone had been rolled across the entrance. The Romans had acquiesced to the suspicions of the priests by fixing the Roman seal over the stone and posting an armed guard.

Sabbath provided one day of respite. Travel and work restrictions stopped everything. But on the first day of the week the emotional waves began again.

It started with Mary of Magdala. Before sun up, she came running into the house where Simon Peter was hiding. "The body is gone. The stone has been taken completely away. That new tomb is empty."

Young John, glanced at the Nazarene's mother, then darted out the door, heading for Joseph's tomb as fast as his young body could fly.

Simon proceeded at a more cautious pace, but soon joined John at the empty opening. Sure enough the stone was laying nearby!

"Joseph's linen shroud is still in there," young John, out of breath from his race, gasped.

Peter was not about to make any more hasty judgements. He looked carefully about. No one was near.

Stooping down into the low opening, he entered the tomb. A single ray from the raising sun pierced the darkness of the tomb. The smell of death still lingered. The linen shroud was laying undisturbed on the shelf left by the excavators. The stains from the tortured corpse were unmistakable. The torn and stained cloth napkin, smelling of myrrh and so recently used by Mary of Magdala, had been used to cover the grotesque and disfigured face. It was folded neatly, laying in a place by itself. Someone had been here!

"I'm getting out of here," he said to John. "This is some kind of a set up. The priests are not satisfied with one crucifixion. We had better not be here when the sun comes up."

They hurried, very quietly, to their safe house.

*****

Peter heard a lot, but saw nothing.

For days Mary of Magdala talked about a visit with a gardener. She talked about two mysterious angelic visitors.

A week later other disciples told about an evening visit. The Nazarene had seemed to materialize in the room. He had talked with them, echoing some of the same teaching about peace that he had spoken about several years before on the shores of Galilee.

Thomas was doubtful. "Unless I place my finger in the nail holes, and my hand in the wound, I won't believe it is Him."

Peter for one, although he was not as dramatic as Thomas, wondered at the impossibility of these fantastic stories.

Then suddenly Thomas did a complete about face. He was a high as a kite. He kept telling Peter that the Nazarene could hear what they were saying.

Peter knew, too well, what the Nazarene had heard him say.

*****

Peter had heard a lot, but still he had seen nothing.

There was nothing left to do but try to get back to the lake, become invisible, try to fit back into the fishing business, and begin to rebuild the old life.

Under cover of darkness, Peter, Thomas, Nathaniel, and Zebedee's sons left Jerusalem to make the journey back to Galilee. Perhaps they would find safety at the lake. The women would be in less danger if they traveled separately. They would come later.

After several days of outfitting the boat, mending unused nets, and packing supplies, it was time to get back to the old life.

"I'm going fishing tomorrow evening," Peter announced. The old partners put their hands together in a contract to the partnerships which had supported them for many years.

As the sun set the boat slipped quietly away from the dock into the night mists of the lake.

As had happened many times, they fished all night and caught nothing. They tried several productive places, but it made no difference. As the daylight painted the sky, a crew of tired fishermen headed for the dock at Capernium. Their storage lockers were dry and empty. This had happened before. It would happen again. Who knows, tomorrow night could be exactly the opposite. A day of rest would be welcome.

The vessel, riding high on the water because of the light load, rounded the point of land protecting the docks at Capernium. A slice of the sun blazed above the eastern Gadarene hills. The still morning waters of Galilee were covered with mist. Squawking gulls escorted the boat into the little bay hoping for a chance to clean up the dockside waters when the fish were cleaned and packed in salt.

On the point of land, a little wisp of smoke curled up in the breathless morning air. A man was standing by a tiny charcoal pit. His figure cast a long shadow in the morning sun.

As Peter's boat came within hailing distance, the stranger began to gesture.

"Do you have any fish," his voice echoed over the stillness of the morning waters.

Obviously, this fellow was hungry for a breakfast. He wanted to roast his meal, rather than depend upon the sun dried fare available in the local market stalls.

"No fish this morning, stranger," Peter called back. "Our boat fish locker is completely empty. You will have to depend upon the market for your breakfast."

They were now getting close enough to hear the fellow clearly.

"Turn around. Turn around." The stranger was pointing back at deeper water.

"But throw your nets out of the other side of your boat."

No one will ever know why Peter did not remember the first time a man near his dock had asked him to turn his boat around and cast nets out of the wrong side of the boat. No one will ever know why Peter did not react negatively to this amateur request. As a professional fisherman, he knew far more than any stranger making ridiculous suggestions. It was an incongruous request.

But for unknown reasons, Peter followed the stranger's suggestion.

It was not far to the place the stranger had suggested. In a few minutes, the nets were prepared for spreading... from the wrong side of the boat.

As the net hit water and the shiny scales of hundreds of fish began to flash towards his boat, the light dawned in Peter's befuddled brain.

This was no stranger. This was the Nazarene! He had done this miracle three years ago.

Peter did not even take time to tell his partners to take command. Grabbing his cloak, he dove into the water, swimming in frantic strokes for the now distant point of land.

Breathing hard, Peter stepped through the rocks covering the bottom of the shore. They hurt his feet, but did not slow him at all. Quickly he pulled his wet coat over his body and ran toward the Nazarene.

The smoke from the little charcoal pit still rose on the still morning air, but the Nazarene did not need any fish. Here was a fish meal, cooked and ready to eat, sizzling on the charcoal.

It was at that moment Peter realized he was alone with the Nazarene.

Why then did the sound of a rooster hit him like a stone. There were no roosters near this point of beach front land. His ears were ringing. He closed his eyes, but in his mind's eye he could clearly see a man, standing in a seamless robe, near an open window, in the darkness of Passover night, and a curtain fluttering in the wind.

The curses and denials that Peter had shouted, rang in his brain like echos from a crime scene. The Nazarene had heard every word. Thomas was right. He hears every word we say.

Peter's reaction was that of a man who had been hit very hard. He staggered and fell, face down, to the sand.

"Peter, do you love me?" the Nazarene asked. The word He used was a common word, used in easy speech, as in I love that game, or I love this place or time, or I loved that girl.

Peter dared not lift his face from the sand. "Yes, Lord. I love you," he replied. But the words of denial were boiling through his consciousness, driving Peter close to madness.

The Nazarene was silent for a few minutes.

"Feed my sheep," He finally said.

Peter slowly raised his head from the sand. Why should this man even want to talk to him? For the first time in weeks, the eyes of the Nazarene met his. There was a great sorrow and love in the Nazarene's eyes. As Peter's gaze involuntarily met the Nazarene's, blinding tears spilled over his cheeks and beard.

"Peter, do you love me?" the Nazarene asked. This question was not the same as the first. The word was a term of familial endearment. A parent might ask a child or a spouse this question after a particularly stressful situation, or vice versa. One might ask this question of a friend if their friendship had been seriously damaged.

The eyes of the Nazarene spoke volumes. They were saying "I love you Peter. I want you as my friend. I want you to stay with Me in this family, this group, this new kingdom."

Peter, for all his good intentions, could not endure that direct gaze. He lowered his eyes but heard his own voice saying, "Yes, Lord, I love you."

After another silence, the Nazarene added further instructions. "Feed my lambs," were His words.

Peter thought of the children who had flocked about the Nazarene. Then he remembered the young servant girl in Jerusalem, the one who had heard Peter utter curses and oaths of denial about any relationship with the Nazarene. How could he ever see her again? Peter's emotions overwhelmed him.

Finally, the Nazarene spoke again. "Peter, do you love me?"

This time the word love was one that was seldom used. It spoke of complete commitment without thought of reward. It spoke of a bond so unbreakable, that nothing, not even death, could ever destroy it. It was a word that described a love beyond the ability of a human creature to give. The Nazarene had used a special term, a rarely used word describing the love that God alone could freely bestow.

The Nazarene was asking Peter to be willing to die for Him!

It was time for complete honesty. Peter felt completely vulnerable to this extraordinary and holy being. There was no room for an impulsive, shoot from the hip response. Only a totally truthful confession would do.

Peter knew himself. The sounds of roosters crowing had crushed all of his self confidence and braggadocio. He was inadequate, and he knew it. To confess to a love commitment on the level of the question still echoing in his ears would have been sinful, at best. How could Peter swear allegiance to this Nazarene when he could not even admit his acquaintance to a couple of street people who he probably would never see again in Jerusalem.

It was a moment of complete honesty. In that moment, Peter recognized the Nazarene as the Christ, the Son of the Living God. The words which he had spoken months ago, not of his own understanding, but dictated by God's Spirit, words which the Nazarene had prophesied would become the Rock upon which a great kingdom, a the new covenant, a living church, would be founded, surfaced out of his memory into his consciousness. Peter now knew that confession to be eternal and true.

"Lord, You alone know my heart." This was the most honest reply he could muster. It was his Creator that he was addressing. An honest confession would be the only offering he could make.

The Nazarene smiled. He reached down to the prostrate man. Grasping his arm, he helped him to his knees, and then to stand. Peter felt a hand brushing the sand from his forehead and then brushing the tears from his cheeks and beard.

"Feed my sheep," was the final instruction.

In that repeated calling, sin was forgiven. Past was forgotten. The weight of betrayal lifted from the shoulders of the fisherman. He felt the arm of the Nazarene encircle is own shoulders. The fate that had greeted his old friend, Judas Iscariot would not befall him. Peter knew a death had occurred, a sacrifice had been made, a penalty had been paid, for every word that he had said. He would never deny his commitment to the Nazarene again.

The Highway

Go ye into all the world... Mark 16:15-17

There is a highway going through Galilee. It is more than two thousand years old. I first saw it as it spills over the little valley above what is known as the Mount of the Beatitudes.

Some of the ancient stones that paved this marvel of Roman engineering still remain in place. In some of the steeper grades, stones are terraced like gentle steps going up or down. Pastures and orchards border it in the Galilean region, but it travels through desert and valley, mountain and riverside, north as far as Rome, and south through the mountainous regions of Megido and central Israel and Jerusalem, eventually to Egypt and Africa. It passes through Galilee, but leads to the entire world in either direction.

Horses and donkey carts, camels and sheep, soldiers and merchants have followed its familiar route for two thousand years. The history of the world has moved over its stones.

This ancient highway is more than a geographic and economic artery. It was over its stones a spiritual experience flowed to reach the ends of the earth.

Most of the leaders of that spiritual revolution were natives to Galilee.

They were drawn from, or sent from the beautiful palm lined shores of that productive little lake in the heart of a Roman occupied country, or from an upper room in Jerusalem, to every land of the earth. Every home, village, city, and nation wherein the stories, healings, miracles, and sacraments generated by the Nazarene in three short years at Galilee are celebrated, is connected through that ancient highway to the little synagogue in Capernium, the hillsides surrounding that lake, and the gentle waves lapping at its shores.

He loved this place!

He loved the people who lived there!

They were simple people. Fishermen, tax collectors, widows, teenagers, senior citizens, soldiers, prostitutes, caravan workers, tent makers, wine makers, shepherds, inn keepers. Simple people who did not have the advantages of birth, education, or social position.

They heard the message given to Simon Peter who was charged with the task of feeding the lost lambs and sheep of the world. They too, were called to share the news.

They stepped away from their comfort, the quiet existence, and the security of their established lives, onto the stones of the highway.

Some traveled north into Europe, Italy, and Great Brittan. Some traveled east into Persia and India. Some traveled south into Egypt and Africa. Wherever a highway could lead them, wherever a ship could carry them, wherever a camel caravan could cross, wherever their feet could step, they were compelled to travel.

Firsthand, they experienced the blessed prophecies of the Nazarene who had told them they would be persecuted for righteousness sake, but to rejoice and be exceedingly glad, for so had the prophets been persecuted before them.

All, but John, the teenager, died martyrs deaths. And in the moment of their deaths, they knew the peacemaker's promise.

They wrote letters, blessed by God Himself, that survive to our instruction today.

The new prayer addressing the great and terrible Jehovah as Our Father, or Abba, followed that road and spread along the corridors of civilization, until it is repeated daily, hourly, perhaps every minute, in every country on the planet.

The prayer for forgiveness equal to our willingness to forgive continues to change men and women internally and then empowering them to become instruments of change in the lives of others.

The sermons preached on those shores continue to be quoted in every language in the world.

Crucified, thrown to wild beasts, torn asunder, boiled in oil, shipwrecked, the Galileans rejoiced, and in that rejoicing, conquered every heathen ideology and despotic tyrant that ever lived. In the moments when from a logical standpoint, they were weakest, or about to be obliterated from the earth, they proved to be the strongest. The strange kingdom of heaven was and is even now being proven to be far more real and eternal that any military, political, social or economic system devised by the mind of human beings.

The Nazarene survived the dark ages and crusades, various reformations, the age of enlightenment, despotic kings and kingdoms, tyrannic dictators, attempted genocide, enlightened but godless societies and democracies, the industrial revolution, a century of world wars, the atomic age, the spoiling of the creations of nature in this planet. He is like salt or light.

The inverted philosophy of becoming great by being humble, by becoming rich by becoming poor, by becoming powerful by being meek, has survived every crisis of human social endeavor. The teachings and sermons given on those hills and that mountain remain untouched and unchanged. The eternal sound still ascends to the heavens.

And standing on the horizon, on that highway into the world, stands the Nazarene.

Simon Peter and Thomas would tell you that He has heard everything you have said and seen everything you have done..

Andrew would tell you that He is someone who can satisfy your thirst.

The quiet woman would tell you that He only wants to save you from destruction, too.

The fisherman's widow would tell you He can comfort you and grant you eternal life.

In spite of human corruption of religion, the thousands of steeples that surround the world point silently to Him.

The cobble stones that depart from Galilee, over that little draw between the gentle orchards and pastures arising from the lake shore, beckon.

With the men and women of Galilee, a journey awaits.

ABOUT THE AUTHOR

Monte Fast has served as a Pastor, Christian Educator, Bible College Instructor, and now directs a faith based human services program in rural northern Nevada.

He has studied, traveled, and taught Bible History and Geography as a life long interest and avocation. He has made two trips to the Holy Land. Over the past twenty years, he has experienced first hand the places described in *Stranger By The Lake.* Now he has committed some of these experiences to written form.

His formal education is in church music, but his life's calling has been to share his stories

His lectures and sermons based upon his studies and travels are in demand in several denominations. Many of these stories and ideas had their beginnings around campfires during youth camps and conferences. His greatest joy is seeing another generation of teachers and ministers take form. He finds satisfaction in creating leaders, thereby multiplying the influence of those who first shared these stories with him when he was a young man.

One of his favorite subjects is to offer dramatic interpretations of various personalities from the Bible. Helping young and old empathize their own struggles through the victories and defeats of religious heros and villains changes lives

As a teacher he knows that people tend to learn from people. His stories, first presented in scripture, involve actual people experiencing truth. We learn from these people.

He has written for church publications and edits a human services newsletter that reaches a national mailing list of about 5,000 subscribers. . He has also written and produced several religious dramas as well as composed several songs.

Printed in the United States
117037LV00001B/175-258/A

9 781420 871135